THE SLEEPOVER GANG

Louise   Jo   Charlie   Alex

Jo, a ghost fanatic, has a very strange
story to tell in her *dungeon* basement.

Alex is laid back and easy-going, except when it
comes to a boy called Mick.

Charlie has a passion for junk food and horses.
She's not sure ghosts even exist.

Louise loves sleepovers,
but she's terrified of ghost stories!

Also available in the Sleepover series

The Snowed-in Sleepover
The Haunted Hotel Sleepover
The Camp Fire Sleepover

The Secret Room Sleepover

Sharon Siamon

Hodder
Children's
Books

a division of Hodder Headline plc

To Jeff

Copyright © 1997 Sharon Siamon
Chapter head illustration © Claudio Berni

First published in Great Britain in 1997
by Hodder Children's Books

The right of Sharon Siamon to be identified as the Author of
this Work has been asserted by her in accordance with the
Copyright, Designs and Patents Act 1988.

10 9 8 7 6 5 4 3

A CIP catalogue record for this book is available
from the British Library

ISBN 0 340 67276 5

Typeset by Palimpsest Book Production Limited,
Polmont, Stirlingshire

Printed and bound in Great Britain by
Clays Ltd, St Ives plc

Hodder Children's Books
a division of Hodder Headline plc
338 Euston Road
London NW1 3BH

One

'What's the scariest thing you've ever seen?'

Jo plopped down on an old sofa cushion and peered at her three friends in the dim light. Louise was cross-legged on another cushion, teasing the cat in her lap with a strand of her long fair hair. Charlie was propped on one elbow on an old camping mattress, munching popcorn. Alex, tall and curly-haired, was standing in the light from the tiny window near the ceiling, juggling three soft balls.

All four were in the dungeon, a dark part of the basement in Jo's 150-year-old house. It was a perfect place for secret get-togethers.

'The scariest thing I've ever seen is my brother's face when he's eating,' Charlie groaned. 'He never shuts his mouth when he chews. Ugh!' She rolled over on her back and sighed. 'That's why I love this dungeon. I can get away from jelly-face Jason.'

1

'But remember the spiders when we first came down here?' Alex laughed. 'You couldn't see the walls for spiderwebs.'

'Remember when we found the dungeon?' Charlie said. 'It was so weird – just because one of your juggling balls rolled behind the furnace.'

To get to the dungeon, you went down a long, narrow flight of stairs from Jo's kitchen, ducked behind the furnace, and crawled through a low opening in a thick stone wall. When the four of them discovered the small square room, no one had been in it for over fifty years. It had once been a coal cellar, and so it was pitch black, dirty and full of spiders.

Now it was cosy with old cushions and a rug. They had taken the boards off the small window and washed the grimy glass. It was their place, soundproof, parent-proof, brother- and sister-proof.

'Your brother Jason isn't so bad,' Louise told Charlie. 'It's just his name. JASON.' She shuddered and buried her face in the cat's soft fur. 'It always reminds me of those horror movies. They're the scariest things I've ever seen.'

'But I wasn't talking about movies, or TV shows,' Jo explained. 'I mean, what's the really, truly scariest thing you've ever seen with your own eyes? Everybody knows horror movies aren't real.'

'They make me laugh,' Alex snorted. 'All those special effects and fake blood . . . it's corny!' She gathered her juggling balls in one hand and lurched around the dim, low-ceilinged room with her arms outstretched. 'I'm coming to get you, Louise . . .'

'Stop it!' Louise screamed.

Alex grinned and flopped on a cushion. 'For truly horrible,' she said, 'it has to be real blood. Let me tell you about what happened to my Uncle Ted. Last summer, at the cottage, we had all gone to bed, and only Uncle Ted's candle was still burning, upstairs in the loft.

'Suddenly we heard this terrible scream, and Uncle Ted came tearing down the ladder. His foot was dripping blood. My mother lit the lantern and we all watched as he peeled off his bloody, dripping sock. I thought he must have cut his toes off, or something . . .' Alex stared around at them. 'It was worse.'

'What?' Louise burst out.

'When he took off his sock,' Alex said, 'there were all these black things on his foot, mixed with blood. Some were still

3

wriggling between his toes, but some had sucked so much blood they had burst.'

Jo winced. 'Bloodsuckers? How did they get inside his sock and shoe?'

'Yuck . . .' Charlie buried her face in the cushion.

'Uncle Ted had gone swimming in the afternoon,' Alex said. 'He put his socks and shoes on to walk up to the cottage and then we made dinner, and played cards, and he didn't take his shoes off until he went to bed.'

'I really wish you hadn't told that story,' Charlie groaned. 'Now I'll never be able to go swimming at your cottage.'

'It's a great story,' Jo sighed. '*The Case of the Bloodsoaked Sock.* But the ending was too ordinary – the blood came from leeches. The stories that really scare me are the ones where weird things happen that nobody can explain.'

Jo's voice was low as she stared around at her three friends. 'My Aunt Diana told me a story that is so terrifying – and she says it's true – that I just can't stop thinking about it. It makes me shiver every time I remember the way she described it – the look on her face.' Jo's dark blue eyes were huge.

'Well, tell us,' Charlie said, stuffing more popcorn in her mouth.

'It happened when she was young, like us,' Jo began, then stopped suddenly and frowned. 'Wait a second, someone's calling.'

'Josephine, are you back in there?'

Jo groaned. She hated being called 'Josephine'.

'It's only Heater,' Jo told her friends. She got even by calling her big sister 'Heater' instead of Heather. 'What do you want?' she yelled. Communications had to be shouted through the thick cellar walls.

'It's your turn to pick up the dog poop in the back yard.' Jo's family had a large puppy called Avalanche, or Ava for short.

'I'll do it later,' Jo called.

'No, now,' Heather bellowed. 'I have to cut the grass before I can go out.'

'In a minute . . .' Jo shouted.

'NOW,' Heather roared. 'If you're not out here in one second, I'm coming in to get you.'

'Ignore her,' Jo shrugged. 'She's too afraid of cobwebs to come near this place.'

'Go on, then,' Louise urged. 'Tell us about your Aunt Diana.'

But at that second there was a thumping

5

on the pipes outside the dungeon. Even Charlie jumped.

Jo just sighed. 'That's my mum's signal that there's a phone call for one of us,' she said. 'She bangs on the radiator upstairs.' They had discovered in the early days of the dungeon that the portable phone would not work through the thick stone walls.

'It's probably my dad,' Alex said. 'We have to go shopping.' She stretched her long legs and stood up.

'I've got an idea,' Jo said. 'Why don't we have a sleepover here in the dungeon, tonight, and I'll finish the story. We'll bring candles . . .'

'And food,' Charlie broke in. Her brown eyes danced.

'Great,' Jo went on, 'and sleeping bags. We'll get Mum to hold our calls. Ask your parents and we'll meet back here at seven o'clock.'

Louise looked around the small, shadowy room. 'I don't know about staying here all night,' she said hesitantly. 'You don't think there might be rats or anything, do you?'

'No rats, maybe the odd ghost,' Jo laughed. 'C'mon Louise, it'll be fun.'

Two

Five hours later they were all back in the dungeon.

'I thought you'd never get here.' Jo yanked aside the old flowered curtain so Louise and Alex could duck through the doorway.

'Alex and I were at the mall.' Louise held out a bag. 'We brought stuff to drink. This looks *great*!' She sounded relieved. 'I thought it might be dark and spooky at night.'

Candlelight threw flickering shadows on the old stone walls. In the centre of the dungeon, cushions and sleeping bags were heaped around a low table. Jo had made the table out of an old wood box and covered it with a bright red scarf.

In the middle of the table was a pile of junk food – pretzels, chips, chocolate bars, red liquorice, jelly worms and sour balls.

The feast was surrounded by candles stuck in bottles.

'Jo and I worked all afternoon.' Charlie was propped on one elbow again, eating pretzels. Jo's white cat, Ajax, was curled up beside her, purring.

'I worked, you ate,' Jo laughed. 'I don't know how you can eat so much junk food and stay so thin!'

Alex dropped her armload of sleeping bags, knapsack and pillows with a sigh. 'Is there going to be room for all of us to sleep in here?' she asked.

'Who's going to sleep?' Jo plopped down on a pillow. 'We're going to keep each other up all night telling terrifying tales, aren't we? Well aren't we?' She looked sharply at Alex.

Something was wrong. Usually, their tall, curly-haired friend's green eyes were full of life. Tonight her face was pale and her eyes sad.

'She had a rough day,' Louise whispered to Charlie and Jo.

'I told you, Louise, I don't want to talk about it.' Alex sank down on her pillow and sighed again. The other three stared at her.

'C'mon,' Charlie said, sitting up and flipping her shiny black hair out of her

8

eyes. 'You can tell us. We're your best friends.'

It was true. The four of them had been best friends since the year before, when they found themselves dumped in the same grade-six science group. They were very different – wealthy, popular Jo, Charlie with her Korean beauty and a background of travel to interesting places, artsy Alex and quiet, fair-haired Louise.

But they soon discovered that they made a dynamite team. Working together, they built a model car that ran on methane gas. Their car won first prize at the Science Fair and then exploded at the awards ceremony.

The methane gas filled the school gym with the reek of rotten eggs. None of them would ever forget the sight of everyone dashing from the gym, clutching their noses.

The four of them had collapsed on the gym floor, shrieking with laughter. It was weeks before the smell of rotten eggs faded from the gym. And every time they smelled it, Louise and Charlie, Jo and Alex would shoot each other looks, roll their eyes and explode into laughter again.

That evening in June had bonded them for ever.

'It can't be worse than our car blowing up,' Charlie said, wrinkling her nose. This usually got Alex laughing again.

'This is different,' Alex muttered.

Jo and Charlie looked at Louise for help but she shook her head and shrugged.

'I just hate him,' Alex muttered again, tossing her juggling ball from one hand to the other.

'Him?' Charlie said. 'Which him?'

'Mick.' Alex lifted her frowning face. 'You know how everybody's been saying he likes Sonia?'

'Those are just stupid rumours,' Charlie snorted.

'No they're not,' Alex said miserably. 'It's true. He said he was going to meet me at the mall, and when I got there he was with Sonia. They were laughing and . . . fooling around.'

They all knew that Alex had liked Mick Alonzo since grade three. They could picture the scene at the mall – Mick laughing with Sonia, Alex, watching them.

Jo wrapped her arm around Alex's shoulder. 'Betrayed,' she said. 'That's what you were. Betrayed.'

'What does that mean?' Louise asked.

'It means Alex trusted Mick and believed

10

in him, and he let her down,' Jo looked around at them. 'When someone betrays you, you never feel the same about them again. It's funny, because the story Aunt Diana told me is about being betrayed too.'

Alex's eyebrows shot up. 'Seriously?' she demanded. 'What happened to her?'

'Well,' Jo said slowly, 'it happened a long time ago. But the story is about a man who lets a woman down, and breaks her heart, and then . . .'

'Stop!' Alex said. 'Start at the beginning.'

Three

'Start right back at the beginning,' Charlie agreed, 'and don't leave anything out.'

'But first, let's get settled,' Louise said. She unrolled her sleeping bag and snuggled into it.

'Should we eat now, or save stuff for later?' Jo asked.

'Now,' Louise said.

'Later,' Alex voted.

'Both,' said Charlie, reaching for a handful of chips. 'There's enough good food to last for days down here.'

'The rest of the house seems so quiet and far away,' Louise murmured dreamily. 'It's as if we're all alone.'

'All alone in an old house,' Jo stared at them. 'This is *so weird*! That's exactly what happened to my Aunt Diana.'

'Was the house haunted?' Louise asked quickly. She wiggled deeper into her bag.

'What's the matter, are you scared already?' Charlie laughed. She stretched out again on her old quilt, crunching her chips.

'Jo's telling this story,' Alex suddenly burst out. 'For heaven's sake, let's be quiet and listen!'

They listened. When Jo told a story, you had to listen. Her voice was low and thrilling. It sucked you right into the words, so that you could see pictures in your head and hear people talking.

Jo's voice got lower as she started to speak. The rest of them snuggled deeper in their sleeping bags.

'My Aunt Diana was small for her age, with long dark hair, and blue, blue eyes,' Jo began. 'When she smiled, her eyes glowed, and her mouth curved up at the corners.'

The others glanced at each other. Jo looked exactly like that. She could have been describing herself! They waited to hear more.

Diana was almost thirteen when she went to live in a big old house in the country. She hated to move away from all her friends, but it was a chance for her father to get well.

You see, it was during World War II, and

Diana's father had been sent home with a wounded leg. His leg was healing, but after more than a year his hands still shook and loud noises terrified him.

The doctor said Dad must have quiet and rest if he was ever going to get better. The trouble was that there were three noisy kids in their small apartment – Diana, her eight-year-old sister Rosie, and a new baby, Daniel.

And then, at the beginning of the summer, her father's Uncle William died, and left them a fifteen-room house on the Hudson River. The house was furnished, and Uncle William had even left them his car.

'It's a miracle,' Diana's mother said. 'We'll have seven bedrooms, instead of two!'

'It's a mansion!' Diana's little sister Rosie cheered. 'We're going to live in a mansion.' Rosie had fair soft hair like her mother, and red, rosy cheeks.

'I only visited it once, years ago,' their father smiled, 'but I remember beautiful rose gardens, stretching all the way down to the river. I remember his boat, the *Sea Rider.*'

Diana couldn't help feeling excited about the new house as they packed up to move. Her father would get well there, she was sure.

'Why did Great-uncle William leave the house to us?' she asked, as their train rolled along beside the wide Hudson River.

'I guess there was no one else,' her father smiled. 'He was kind of a strange old duck – spent most of his life sailing around the coast of Florida. He had no wife or children, and not very much money by the time he died. Just this big old house and an old car.'

'A car!' Diana wiggled happily in the seat. Cars were very hard to get during the war. They hadn't owned a car since she was a little girl.

'We'll need a car in the country,' her father squeezed her shoulder. 'We'll be far from any town.'

Just then, the whistle blew. They had arrived at the tiny station of Norville, on the Hudson River.

A sandy-haired boy was waiting for them on the station platform, with the keys to Uncle William's car in his hand.

'I'm Adam Bird,' he told them. 'I looked after Mr Lewis's car while he was away.'

He pointed to an old beat-up Ford. 'She doesn't look like much, but she runs,' he smiled.

Diana noticed that Adam's face flushed

as he talked. He was tall, and thin, but he didn't look much older than she was.

'Can you drive?' she blurted out.

'I'll get a licence next March, when I'm sixteen,' Adam's face flushed again. 'But I know about cars. I've been keeping our truck running while my dad's away in the army.'

'Well, thank you, Adam,' Diana's father said. Diana noticed he let Adam lift the luggage into the car. Dad still wasn't strong.

Adam opened the back door of the car for her and Rosie. 'The old Lewis place hasn't had anybody in it for years,' he said. 'If you need anything . . .' he glanced at Diana and glanced away again quickly, 'my family owns the hardware store in town.'

'Thank you, Adam,' Diana's mother said. 'I'm sure we'll be seeing you.'

Diana found herself wondering about Adam as they drove along the river. He seemed shy, but grown-up at the same time.

'Here's our turn, Dad,' she sang out, just in time. The car skidded into a rutted driveway between two massive stone gate-posts.

Through the trees, they caught glimpses of a huge stone house.

'Is that *our house*?' Rosie breathed in awe, her face pressed against the car window.

Their dad laughed. 'That's it.'

But Diana felt something clutch her heart as they bumped further down the deep, narrow lane. The dark trees almost met overhead. The stone walls looked high and cold. And it was so lonely here – they hadn't seen another person since they left the station.

The lane ended in a thick grove of cedars growing up against the back wall of the immense house. The car rolled around to the front of the house and stopped.

They all got out.

The car doors banged shut, echoing in the silence.

Diana looked up. The house was a huge block of damp grey stone, with a steep roof and two chimneys. The only break in its cold face was a round tower, added on where the kitchen wing met the main house.

Around the pointed roof of the tower, black birds flapped in circles. 'CAW, CAW!' they croaked, as if crying a warning. A torn grey curtain fluttered in the tower window.

Diana felt a shiver. *This* was home?

The place looked completely deserted. Windows were smashed on the main floor and a broken shutter hung by one hinge.

As for the rose garden, nothing was left but a tangle of weeds. At the bottom of the ruined garden, the river flowed, flat and wide. It must be miles to the other side, Diana thought. It was the loneliest view she had ever seen.

'Well,' said her father, 'we might as well go in.'

He limped up the cracked and broken front steps. Ugly green moss had grown between the stones and halfway up the heavy wood door.

Diana saw her father's hand shake as he turned the large, old-fashioned key in the lock. She felt a lump in her throat. Dad was so different from the father she remembered tossing her into the air and catching her in his strong arms, before he went away to war.

What would happen to them in this strange, lonely place? Diana thought with a shudder. Her mother stood holding the baby close in her arms. She hardly seemed to notice where she was, or Dad's shaking hands, or Rosie tugging at his sweater, and whining 'I want in, I want in . . .'

The door creaked open. Rosie burst through under her father's arm and screamed.

'Y-a-a-agh! Spiders!'

Diana stepped through the door into the huge front hall, clamping her hand to her nose as a gust of stale air hit her. It stank of mould and dust, and something worse.

The large rooms off the hall were stuffed with oversized sofas, chairs, tables and heavy wooden cupboards. And Rosie was right. Spiders were everywhere. They froze in the centres of their webs, then scuttled off in all directions.

Spiderwebs covered every surface in a fine grey cloak.

'Oh dear!' Diana's mum said, as they walked from room to room. 'We'll have to clear a spot just so I can put the baby down. Run upstairs, girls, and see if it's any better.'

The main stairs were at one side of the front hall. At the bottom hung a large mirror in a gold frame. As she started up the curving staircase, Diana caught a glimpse of herself, pale and wavering. She had a sudden feeling of dread, as though she were suspended in mid-air.

Rosie rushed past her in a blur of blonde curls. 'Come on,' she cried.

Diana tried to shake off her fear. She could

hear Rosie pounding down the upstairs hall, banging open the bedroom doors.

The musty smell got stronger as she climbed, and the air was hot and heavy. At the top of the stairs the bedrooms opened off a wide hall. Which one was the tower room, Diana wondered, the one with the torn lace curtain?

All the rooms seemed the same. Each one was empty, with a high, old-fashioned bed and a narrow window. Yet, as she walked from room to room, Diana felt as though people had just left. Their presence, like faint perfume, hung in the air. She expected to see someone rise from a dusty bed or run to the window to look out.

All the windows overlooked the ruined garden and the wide, grey Hudson River. Their small panes were covered in spider-webs. Diana shuddered again. She wanted to run from that house of dim light and spiders and never return.

'Let's choose our rooms,' Rosie sang out from somewhere down the hall.

Diana discovered the room she wanted at the end of a small branching hallway. This one at least had two windows. Through one of them, Diana glimpsed a small, vine-covered cottage, close to the river.

Rosie came dashing into the room behind her.

'Oh, I like this one,' she cried. 'It can be mine.'

'You can't have it,' Diana said. 'This is my room.'

'It is not. You just said that because *I* want it,' Rosie stamped her foot.

'Let's go downstairs and let Mum and Dad decide,' Diana said, anxious not to start one of Rosie's tantrums. Since the new baby had arrived, Rosie had a habit of throwing herself on the floor, kicking and screaming until she got her way.

'Come on.' Diana took Rosie's hand and led her out into the hall. 'Look, Rosie, there's even a back stairway to the kitchen.'

Rosie was impressed. She'd never seen a house with two sets of stairs. She took a deep breath 'All right,' she said. 'Dad can decide.' They clattered down the narrow, twisting back staircase to the kitchen.

'We'll toss a coin for it,' their father said, when he'd heard both sides. He dug a penny out of his pocket. 'Heads, it's Diana's room, tails, it's Rosie's room.'

Diana won the toss.

'There are lots more rooms to choose from, Rosie,' her mother said. 'Daniel will sleep down here, with us, so I can hear him if he cries. We'll make a bedroom in the den until your father's leg is better.'

For a moment, Rosie looked like she was going to throw herself on the floor and scream. Instead, she stuck her tongue out at Diana and stomped off up the back stairs.

Diana found an old lamp and carried it up to her. By now, the light was too dim in the hallway to see.

Grumbling, Rosie chose the room at the end of the hall. 'It's as far away from you as I can get,' she pouted.

Diana went back down for a scrub brush and pail of soapy water.

'What's the smell in this house?' she asked, wrinkling her nose.

'Maybe some small animal died in the walls,' her father sighed. 'We're going to have a job making this place liveable.'

'Rosie and I can do our rooms,' Diana said. 'Don't worry.'

'I'll help you clean your room, and then you can help me,' she told Rosie.

'No!' Rosie stamped her foot again. 'I'm not helping you with anything!' She was still mad about losing the big room.

'But Rosie, there's only one pail.'

'Then I want it,' Rosie frowned and stuck

out her bottom lip. 'You can't have every-thing first.'

Diana handed her the pail, and brush, 'Take them,' she sighed. 'And try not to spill water all over everything.'

She heard Rosie muttering and banging away down the hall. She would wait until Rosie got into a mess and then offer to help again.

In the meantime, she could peel off some of the loose wallpaper in her own room. She dragged a tall floor lamp up the stairs and plugged it in behind the bed. It threw a large patch of light on the wall. That would be a good place to start, she thought.

Without knowing why, Diana began to feel a bit happier. Maybe it was the idea of having her own room. No Rosie. No baby Daniel. Peace and quiet at last. She liked peeling off the ancient green wallpaper. It ripped off in long, satisfying strips.

A few minutes later, her fingers felt a groove, running crosswise. The paper seemed stuck tight over the groove. Diana ran her fingers along it, and found a corner. Another groove ran up and down.

Diana stood back, staring. There was a door under there. A door, papered over.

She ran her finger all around the shape

of the door again. It was a small door, not much higher than her head. Maybe an old closet, or an attic, Diana thought. But why would anyone paper over it, seal it shut?

There seemed to be no door handle, but there was a hole where one should be! Diana could feel the dent under her hand when she pressed at the wallpaper.

'What are you doing?' Rosie stood in the doorway.

'I'm taking off the loose wallpaper,' Diana said. Suddenly she didn't want Rosie to know about the sealed door. It was her room, her secret. She would wait until Rosie had gone to bed to open it.

A loud banging on the radiator pipes made them all jump.

'Jo, can you hear me?' Jo's mother bellowed from the top of the basement stairs. 'Charlie's brother Jason called. He said to tell you he would get even.'

They looked at Charlie. Her face was lit with laughter. 'I put cracker crumbs in his sleeping bag,' she chuckled. 'He's going to a sleepover too, at Andrew's. I'll bet he had fun getting those crumbs out.'

'Thanks for the message, Mrs Lewis,' she called to Jo's mum.

'There's a fresh pizza at the top of the stairs for you,' the hollow voice boomed back. 'Jo, your dad and I are going out, but Heather's here. Have a good time.'

Four

The pizza was delicious – double cheese and pepperoni. They each had three slices, washed down with cola and orange pop.

'Your mother is amazing,' Charlie sighed happily, reaching for the dish of jelly worms.

'Dad is the pizza maker,' Jo said. 'His secret ingredient is dill pickles.'

'I wish you hadn't told me that,' Charlie groaned. 'I hate dill pickles.'

'Aren't you worried about what Jason is going to do to get even?' Louise asked.

'Never!' Charlie laughed. 'He has no imagination when it comes to playing tricks on me. I can spot them coming a week away.'

'It seems kind of mean to put crumbs in his sleeping bag,' Louise said.

'Are you kidding?' Charlie's eyebrows shot up. 'You've obviously never had a little brother. His whole purpose in life is to bug me.'

'But he's so cute . . .' Alex said.

'Well, I'll bet Diana's sister Rosie was cute too, and look at how she drove Diana crazy!'

'Let's get back to the story,' Louise said. 'What happened that night? Did she get into the secret room?'

'Is everybody ready?' Jo asked, wiping her hands on a paper napkin. 'The next part is kind of, well . . . interesting.'

Jo's voice grew quiet again. She leaned forward to tell the story, the candlelight gleaming in her eyes.

Diana waited in the darkness until the house was quiet. Then, she slipped out of bed and turned on the lamp. It threw long, spooky shadows up the walls.

'I'm going to look behind the door,' she whispered to herself. 'There's nothing to be afraid of . . .'

She inched her way across the floor, almost holding her breath. The bare wood boards were cold under her feet. If only the floor wasn't so creaky! She didn't want to wake her parents, downstairs.

Earlier that day, she had hidden a butcher knife in her top drawer. She eased open the drawer, and felt for the knife under her clothes. There it was – long and sharp enough to cut through the layers of stiff old paper covering the door.

But first, she would cut a hole where the door handle had been, and look inside.

She dragged the lamp closer to the end wall so she could clearly see the door's outline, and felt down the right side for the dent. There it was!

Diana stabbed the knife through the paper and cut around the hole. Then she caught her breath with a gasp. A horrible stench came from the black hole, like an evil blast of air from an open grave.

Diana remembered her father's words, 'There must be something dead in the walls.'

'I'm going to look,' she told herself again. But she was trembling in her thin nightgown as she pulled the lamp even nearer.

Holding her nose, she bent over, cupped her hand around the hole, and pressed her eye to the opening.

It was not a closet. There was a curving staircase behind the door. Diana could see streaks of moonlight on the stairs from a high-up window. There must be a secret room at the top of the stairs!

There was something . . . fluttering in the moonlight, then a horrible flapping sound. Something skittered against the other side of the eyehole . . . Diana jerked back, clutching for the lamp.

A sudden scrabbling at her own bedroom door made her swing wildly around, every atom of her being tingling with terror. The door swung slowly open. A white shape was silhouetted against the black opening.

'Diana . . .' a quavering voice came from the white shape. 'I can't sleep.'

It was only Rosie. Diana sighed with relief. Rosie was standing in a hand-me-down nightgown that covered her feet and dragged on the floor. Mother, Diana thought in a quick burst of anger, was too busy with her baby brother Daniel to fix up her old clothes for Rosie.

She felt a huge wave of pity for Rosie. When her dad was away in the army, she had looked after Rosie while Mother worked. It looked like she would still be looking after her.

'Go back to bed, Rosie-Posie,' she said. 'Come on, I'll tuck you in.' She tried to control the shaking in her voice and body.

'Why are you out of bed? Why do you sound so funny? And what's that yucky smell?' Rosie fired the questions as she shuffled into the room.

'Ugh! It smells worse than Daniel's diarrhoea in here!'

'It's just this old house,' Diana said. 'You should get back to bed.'

'No. You're doing something in here. I know you are. I heard you dragging stuff around.' Rosie shuffled forward and almost tripped over the knife on the floor. She stared at it and then turned a shocked face to Diana.

'What are you doing with the butcher knife?'

It was useless now to try to keep her out of it, Diana knew. Rosie was like a dog with a bone when she thought Diana was trying to hide something from her.

'There's a door,' she explained, tipping the light forward so Rosie could see. 'And stairs, leading up. Someone sealed up the door with wallpaper. I was just cutting out the hole where the doorknob used to be. That's where the smell is coming from.'

'Are you going to go up there?' Rosie's eyes stared at her. 'Tonight?'

'I don't know,' Diana said. She felt herself

shuddering. 'There's something in there. I felt it brush the door.'

'We could call for Mother,' Rosie suggested, her eyes enormous.

'We can't,' Diana said. 'We'll wake Dad. He's supposed to rest.'

She would have to get Rosie back to bed and deal with this herself.

But Rosie refused. 'I'll scream if you make me go back to bed,' she announced. 'And that will wake everybody up.'

'Then hold the light,' Diana said. 'I'm going to try to open the door.'

Rosie held the lamp close to the wall, while Diana wiggled the knife back and forth in the crack, loosening the old glue. 'There,' she gasped. 'I think it's coming unstuck.'

Carefully, she reached her fingers through the door hole, trying to get a grip. 'I'm going to pull,' she told Rosie. 'Whatever you do,' she whispered fiercely, 'don't drop the lamp, and don't scream.'

She gave a mighty yank. The door came loose with a tearing sound. It swung open. Something flapped into her face. Diana threw herself backwards. More of the flapping things swooped towards them, silent and horrible. Rosie dropped the lamp to clamp both hands over her screaming mouth and Diana caught it just as it hit the bare wood floor and blinked out.

They both dived under the bed in the blackness, clutching each other.

'Something . . . dived . . . at my hair,' Rosie stuttered. 'I want Mother.'

Diana hugged her little sister's body close. She could feel her sweaty forehead and thudding heart. 'I think they're bats,' she said. 'Just bats. We must have disturbed them.'

'B-but how did b-bats get in there?' Rosie snuffled.

'I think there must be a room up there, with an open window,' Diana whispered. 'I'm going to look.' She felt for the lamp cord, and pulled the lamp towards her. She fumbled for the switch in the darkness.

'There,' Diana said, as the bulb blinked, and flickered and then shone brightly. 'You stay here. I'm going to open the window in this room. Maybe the bats will fly out.'

She reached up on the bed for a pillow. Bats had good sonar, she knew, but they still liked to dive at people's heads.

Holding the pillow over her head she ran to open the gable windows wide.

Sure enough, a stream of winged creatures flapped out into the moonlight, as if glad to be released.

'You can come out now, Rosie,' she called to Rosie under the bed. 'Our visitors have gone.'

Rosie's face was pale as she struggled out from under the bed. 'Why didn't they take their smell with them?'

Holding the lamp high, they tiptoed to the door in the wall. The lamplight shone on the stair treads. They were streaked white with bat droppings.

'It must lead to the tower room,' Diana said breathlessly.

'Are you really going up there?' Rosie whispered.

Diana nodded. 'First, let me tie up your nightgown. The floor doesn't look very clean.'

It wasn't. They edged up the short flight of narrow, winding steps, trying to avoid the worst of the slimy white droppings.

At the top they stood and gasped.

The room had once been richly furnished, with red velvet chairs and a carved dressing table with a large gold-edged mirror. There was an elegant four-poster bed, hung with more velvet. This had once been a beautiful bedroom, hidden away in the tower.

Now, all was dust and decay. The bats had been using the tower room as a roost for many long years. The floor was stained white, and so was the back of an old-fashioned love-seat.

'Pew,' Rosie said. 'I didn't know bats smelled so bad.'

Diana stepped slowly and carefully across the wood floor, and closed the window. The lace curtain hung in shreds.

'Look!' Rosie whispered.

Diana turned. Rosie was standing in front of the dressing table, holding a piece of notepaper and a beautiful pair of silver scissors with long, sharp blades. The back of her head was reflected in the mirror.

For a split second, Diana glimpsed something else in the mirror. A wavering shape, reaching, surrounding Rosie's curly head. A chill terror swept through Diana.

'Put those scissors down!' she said sharply.

Rosie, startled, let the paper flutter out of her hand. But she gripped the scissors tighter.

'Why?' Rosie asked. 'I'm just looking at them.'

The wavering shadow in the mirror had

vanished with Diana's sharp cry. There was just the reflection of Rosie in the glass. Rosie in her long white nightgown, clutching the silver scissors.

'I'm going to wash these up, and have them,' Rosie said, snapping the scissors. 'I can use them for my paper dolls. They have nice sharp points, so I can get around the corners.'

'No,' Diana said, her voice still high. 'You're going to put those scissors back and we're going to go downstairs and shut the door.'

The chill had left her numb, almost unable to move. Someone, or something, she was sure, did not want the room to be disturbed.

'Why are you always so bossy!' Rosie whined. 'You're not my mother, you know. I can take the scissors if I want to.'

'No you can't,' Diana said, furiously. 'They don't belong to you.' She reached for the scissors, and Rosie backed away, holding them high over her shoulder.

'Give them to me,' Diana hissed, moving forward.

'No!' Rosie said, backing away.

Diana lunged for the scissors.

Rosie tripped and fell.

To Diana, she seemed to fall in slow

motion. Diana saw her sister's arm bend under her, saw the sharp glint of scissors, saw a shower of red.

In horror, she moved forward to the crumpled heap of Rosie's body.

Five

'Rosie!' Diana's voice was hoarse with terror.

She reached out for her little sister, but something seemed to be holding her back. It was like a bad dream where she tried to run but her feet were clamped to the floor.

Diana fought the force in the room, an evil, angry force that surrounded her. She battled through it to clutch her sister's body close.

'I'm all right,' Rosie shook her head. 'I tripped – on my nightgown, I guess.'

'Are you hurt? Those scissors! I thought you fell on them—' Diana felt the folds of the bulky nightgown. There was no blood, no wound.

On the floor, the scissors lay gleaming in a sliver of moonlight.

'There they are,' Rosie cried, reaching for the scissors. 'What's that mark on the floor?'

Under the scissors, on the bare floor boards, was a dark stain.

'Don't touch,' Diana said quickly. She was so sure she had seen bright red, the colour of blood. But the stain was dark, dark brown. If it had once been a bloodstain, it was very old.

'Let's get out of here,' Diana shuddered, gripping Rosie's hand.

'I want my scissors,' Rosie said stubbornly. She wriggled out of Diana's grip.

'Rosie, please leave them. I think they're meant to stay here,' Diana begged.

'You just want them, but they're mine,' Rosie bent to pick them up.

The *thing*, the force, hovered nearer. Diana caught a glimpse of a face in the mirror, twisted with fury.

She must, at all costs, get Rosie out of here and shut the door. She could return the scissors later.

'All right. But come quickly,' she urged. Rosie bent, clutched the silver scissors in one hand, the piece of paper in the other. 'Here!' she thrust the paper at Diana. 'What does it say?' Diana's voice sounded hollow as she read,

'Meet me at the boat house. Do not fail.'

The printing was in large, old-fashioned letters.

With a shudder, Diana threw the paper on the desk. Then, gathering all her strength, she dragged Rosie out of the room and down the stairs. She leaned against the door, forcing it back into place.

'Look, Diana.' Rosie held the scissors up to the lamplight. 'They don't even need polishing like our old knives and spoons. They're shiny already.'

'That's just it, Rosie. They shouldn't be shiny,' Diana said quickly. 'They should be black from lying shut up in that room. I don't want you to play with the scissors. Promise you won't.'

'You're just jealous. You always want the best things,' Rosie pouted. 'And when I get something good, you say it's no good. I hate you.'

What on earth was happening to them? She and Rosie had been so close before baby Daniel was born. Now, Rosie hated her.

'Let's stop fighting about the scissors,' Diana said. 'Can I sleep in your room? It smells so awful in here.'

'Well,' Rosie put her head on one side and considered. 'Maybe. If you're nice to me.'

'I promise,' Diana said.

They tiptoed down the creaking hall to Rosie's room. It was amazing, Diana thought, that all the noise they had made in the tower room hadn't wakened her parents. The tower room must be over the kitchen with its high, beamed ceiling.

Here, in the main hall, every tiny creak of their footsteps would be magnified downstairs. She pushed the door to Rosie's room open softly.

Soon they were settled in Rosie's big, four-poster bed, and Rosie was asleep.

Diana had trouble falling asleep. There was danger in this house. She had felt such power and wickedness in that tower room.

Outside, the wind moaned in the trees behind the house. Shadows of moonlight played through the window. An old shutter creaked and banged.

Tomorrow, Diana thought, she would go and look for the boat house that was mentioned in the note. Perhaps it held a clue to the mysteries of the house.

There was another enormous bang on the pipes outside the dungeon. All four of them jumped out of their sleeping bags. Ajax the cat leapt into the air, her tail straight up. Louise stuffed her pillow in her mouth to muffle a scream.

'There's a phone call for Alex,' came a faraway voice.

'It's just Heater,' Jo relaxed. 'No calls!' she bellowed back. 'Leave us alone.'

'This guy has already called three times,' Heather bellowed back. 'Why don't you tell your dumb boyfriends you don't want them to call?'

'Did he say who it was?' Jo shouted.

'Someone called Mick,' Heather's voice came back. 'Listen, I'm going out, so if you want this call, come and get it now!'

They all looked at Alex, who shook her head fiercely.

'No!' they all shouted together.

'Okay. I'm out of here. I'll be back before Mum and Dad get home. Don't tell, all right?'

Jo was silent.

'All right?' Heather called again.

'Sure. Fine, Heater. Go.' Jo roared. 'Have a good time.'

Louise brushed back her fine blonde hair and looked up at Jo. 'Will you tell?' she asked.

'That depends,' Jo's mouth curved up in a grin. 'I might need her to do me a favour some day.' She smoothed Ajax's ruffled fur. 'So I probably won't tell that she went out and left us all alone.'

Six

'So, now your big sister has gone out,' Charlie said cheerfully. 'That means we are totally alone here. And I think this house has secrets, too.'

Louise shuddered. 'Don't talk like that . . .' she said.

Jo was gazing thoughtfully at Alex. 'Mick must really want to talk to you,' she said, 'if he called three times . . .'

'Well, I don't want to talk to him – ever again,' Alex muttered. She threw the ball in her hand against the wall, and then went over to pick it up, hiding her face from her friends. They shared glances.

'Go on with the story,' Alex said. 'It's much more interesting than stupid old Mick.'

The other three glanced at each other. They didn't believe Alex for one second.

42

'Okay, snuggle in, guys,' Jo said. 'It gets better. We had Diana and Rosie in Rosie's room at the end of the hall, remember? And Diana is having a hard time falling asleep, after what she'd seen in the secret room.'

They nodded.

'The first thing Diana knew, it was morning.' Jo's voice sank again, and the candlelight gleamed on her face as the three of them cuddled closer in their sleeping bags to listen.

When Diana opened her eyes, the bedroom was filled with pale light. Rosie was still asleep. Her cheeks were flushed and one hand was clutching the silver scissors close to her heart.

Diana gasped, and reached over her sister's body, careful not to startle her. Gently, gently, she tried to untangle Rosie's fingers from their grip on the scissors.

'What are you doing? They're mine!' Rosie's eyes shot open.

'Yes, I know.' Diana forced her voice to be calm. 'But it's not safe to sleep with scissors. Listen, I want you to hide the scissors in a secret place – but not your bed. If you'll do that, I promise not to look for them, or tell Mum.'

'Okay,' Rosie said. 'Promise, cross your heart, and hope to die?'

'And eat red ants, if I tell a lie,' Diana said. 'I'm going to get dressed and go out, and then you can hide the scissors.'

She tiptoed back to her room to get some clothes.

The door to the staircase and secret room was still closed, but the sharp smell of bats made her gag. Quickly, Diana scooped up her clothes – a red skirt, a warm jersey and some clean socks and underwear – and dashed down the back stairs to the kitchen.

The kitchen was silent and cold. Her parents must still be asleep. Shivering, Diana dressed quickly and headed for the front door. As she passed the baby's room she could hear Daniel cooing and gurgling. He was safe in his crib.

Diana pulled open the creaky front door and stepped outside. She wanted to go down to the river and find the boat house before anyone else was up.

A big barge was floating by in the middle of the river. It was so far away the men on board were just tiny stick figures.

As Diana hurried through the tangle of tall grass and weeds, she saw a dark

44

shape moving down by the river's edge. It seemed to be an old woman, wrapped in a black shawl.

Diana tried to hurry forward to meet her, but the thorns of an old rose bush caught at her skirt. She pricked her fingers on the long sharp thorns trying to yank it free. By the time her dress was untangled, the woman was gone.

Diana ran to the river's edge. A dirt path, worn smooth by many feet, ran along the water. She looked up and down the path, but there was no one there.

Diana followed the path to the left until she came to a sagging boat house. It was standing part in the water, and part on land. A broken wood sign over the door said *Sea Rider*.

'Great-uncle William's boat!' Diana breathed. When she peered through a window she could see that the floor was open to the river, with just a narrow walkway around three sides. The whole boat house leaned dangerously to one side.

Whoever had met at the boat house, long ago, had left no clue. The river flowed, smooth and wide, as though it had seen nothing, or wouldn't tell.

'Di-a-na!' She heard someone call her name. Diana shoved her way back through the weeds and brambles to the house. Her mother stood on the front porch with Daniel in her arms.

'I saw someone, walking along the river,' Diana panted as she ran up the steps, '. . . an old lady. Did you see her, Mum?'

Her mother snuggled her face into Daniel's cheek. 'I didn't see anyone but you. Have you been having a nice time in the garden?'

'It's full of weeds and thorns!' Diana said.

'But the river is beautiful, isn't it?' Her mother smiled. 'We'll have to clear a path so we can go down and swim.'

The river was too big to be beautiful, Diana thought.

'But this morning, we have to drive into town,' her mother went on. 'We need paint, and wallpaper, and we have to find someone to help us fix up the house. Maybe that nice young man who met us at the station. What was his name?'

'Adam,' Diana said.

'He looked strong, and hard-working,' her mother nodded. 'Have you thought about how you'd like your room?'

'I thought . . . maybe I'll share a room with Rosie, after all,' Diana stammered. The thought of sleeping next to the hidden doorway of the secret room made her cold with fear. How could her mother not see the danger all around them?

Her mother beamed, kissing Daniel's fuzzy blonde head again. 'That's nice, dear. One less room to clean up and decorate.'

Bird's hardware store was a small building on the main street of Norville. It was a very small town, just a couple of stores and a boat-repair place on the river.

Adam was nowhere to be seen. There was a sharp-faced woman behind the counter.

'So you're going to fix up the old Lewis place,' the woman said. She was smiling, Diana noticed, but her eyes were the colour of grey flint. 'Are you planning to *live* there, year round?'

'It's our home, for now,' Diana's father nodded.

An old man hobbled in from the back room. 'I thought I heard Will Lewis in here!' he exclaimed and stared the family up and down. 'But they said William was dead, drowned in that fool boat of his.'

'I'm David Lewis, his nephew,' Diana's father introduced himself to the old man.

'So Will left the place to you,' the old man chuckled. 'Well, that sure put my daughter-in-law's nose out of joint. This here is my daughter-in-law, Shirley. She always wanted to buy that house, didn't you, Shirl?'

The woman's flinty eyes shot sparks. 'It's none of your business what I wanted.'

'Well, you did. You wanted that big house awful bad. And now you're not going to get it . . .' He laughed in a nasty way, and then peered at Diana. 'You look like a Lewis too. Same black hair, like a crow's wing. Just be careful, little one.'

Diana stared back at him. 'Careful of what, sir?' she stammered.

'I wouldn't make too many changes to that house,' he cackled again. '*She* wouldn't like it.'

'Stop your nonsense,' the woman said.

The old man put his finger up to his lips. 'She doesn't like it when you change things around. Likes the house to stay just the way it was when . . .'

'I said, stop it!' The woman took the old man by the arm and hustled him to the back of the store. They could hear a door bang and then hurrying footsteps as she returned. 'He's old,' she said. 'He talks a lot of nonsense about the past.'

She tried to smile. 'Here's the paint

samples and the wallpaper book. Take your time.'

Diana and Rosie chose pale blue wallpaper for their room. As they carried their supplies out to the car, Adam appeared out of nowhere. He nodded shyly, and helped them load the car.

He patted the old Ford. 'How's she running?'

'Fine,' Diana's father smiled. 'You looked after her very well.'

Adam looked pleased. 'My mother said you might need me out at the house?'

They all nodded.

'I'll be there this afternoon.' Adam flashed a shy grin. 'Well, goodbye.' He turned sharply and disappeared into the store.

'He seems much friendlier than his mother, Shirley,' Diana's mother sighed. 'I guess she must be very disappointed about buying the house. She must have been waiting for years!'

'But why wouldn't she want things moved around?' Diana asked.

'Just an old local superstition,' Diana's father said. 'There used to be some strange stories about our house. Uncle William would never tell me the details, but I guess other people heard them too.'

He smiled at Diana. 'Anyway, they knew right away you're a Lewis,' he said.

'Tell me about Great-uncle William,' Diana begged her father, as they drove up the bumpy, overgrown lane. 'Did he drown in the river?'

'Oh, no,' her father shook his head. 'His boat went down in a storm off Florida. He hasn't lived around here for years.'

'Why?' Diana pressed.

'Well, William was born in the gardener's cottage, down by the river. The Lewises were gardeners on this estate. When William made a fortune on the stock market, he bought the big house.

'Then he lost all his money in the stock market crash,' her father went on. 'He closed up the mansion and sailed away in his yacht. That would be almost fifteen years ago.'

'Who lives in the gardener's cottage now?' Diana asked. Her father must mean the vine-covered cottage she'd seen from the window.

'Summer people,' her father said. 'They rent it for the summer, but they aren't here yet.'

'Well,' Diana sighed as the car pulled up in front of the old stone mansion, 'no wonder this place is such a wreck. No one has lived here for fifteen years.'

She gazed up at the small tower window. It glared back at her like a blind, glassy eye.

Diana felt that strange chill again, remembering the old man's warning. They had disturbed things. She had shut the window. Rosie had taken the scissors.

Diana couldn't forget the old man's cackle of laughter. What were the strange stories he knew?

Maybe Adam could tell her, she thought suddenly. The old man must be his grandfather – this afternoon she would ask him.

'I hope Diana is not going to count on Adam,' Alex said. 'You can't trust guys.'

'I agree,' Charlie nodded. 'There's something weird about the way Adam keeps appearing so suddenly.'

Jo grinned. 'You think so, do you?'

'Tell us, Jo,' Louise begged. 'Can she trust him?'

'Wait and see,' said Jo.

'Oh, you're awful—'

Just then, there was a scratching noise at the high-up window. It had got dark while Jo was telling the story, and when they looked up, the window was just a small black square at the top of the wall.

'I hate that window,' Louise said. 'It makes me feel like I'm in some kind of a prison cell.'

'Look,' Alex cried. 'What's that?' She grabbed Louise, who let out a scream.

A hideous gargoyle face was pressed against the glass, then another and another.

Seven

A weird light lit the three frightening faces. The eyeballs bulged. The mouths were stretched into ghastly grins.

Louise clutched Alex's hand.

Charlie stood up. 'Jason! Is that you and your wormy little friends?'

There was a wild burst of laughter from outside.

'Jason!' Charlie bellowed. 'If you're not gone in two seconds, I'm letting Jo's dog out after you. And turn off that flashlight!'

There was another burst of giggles from above and the window went dark.

'I should have known Jason would try to get even,' Charlie groaned.

'Let's rig up a curtain,' Jo said. 'In case they come back.'

'They won't be back,' Charlie shook her head. 'I'm sure they got the brilliant idea to come and scare us on the way to *their* sleepover. They're not allowed to roam around outside after dark.'

'The curtain is still a good idea,' Alex said. '*Anyone* could look in.'

'Let's do it tomorrow,' Charlie said. 'I want to find out what happens to Diana.' She grabbed a handful of red liquorice and collapsed on her quilt. 'Keep going, Jo.'

'We're getting to what I call the *Night of Terror*,' Jo said in a low, thrilling voice. 'Diana has waited all morning for Adam to come. The hours seem to crawl by . . .'

One by one, they settled down again, their thoughts returning to the lonely house by the river, and to Diana, waiting for Adam.

At one o'clock, just like he promised, Adam came bumping down the lane on his bicycle. Diana was watching for him by the kitchen door.

'Hello,' she said.

Adam flushed and got off the bike. He bent to undo his pack behind the seat.

'What's in there?' Diana asked, and the next second wished she could bite her question back. She sounded like a little kid.

'My tools,' Adam said, swinging the pack

on his back. He was wearing work overalls that made him look even taller.

It was not going to be easy to ask him questions, Diana thought. Adam wasn't exactly the talkative type! 'I'll get my dad,' she said.

Adam just nodded, and stood his bike against the side of the house. He looked around with great curiosity.

Diana yanked open the kitchen door. 'Adam's here!' she blurted.

Her father limped forward to greet him. 'Thanks for coming,' he smiled. 'Your young legs will be very welcome. I got a little tired in town this morning.'

Diana saw that Adam was barely listening. His eyes were darting around the kitchen, taking in every detail. He looked up at the high ceiling, and Diana's eyes followed his gaze.

Did she imagine it, or was there a faint outline of a stain in the ceiling plaster? The dark stain on the floor of the secret room must be right above them. What did Adam know about that?

'We'd like to set up our bedroom in the sitting room downstairs,' her father was saying.

'You want to change the rooms?' Adam

gulped. Diana could see the lump in his throat bob up and down.

Her father laughed. 'Listen, I know there's some old story about not changing anything in this house, but I don't believe in old stories.'

Adam's face went from red to white, and back to red again.

'Say something!' Diana wanted to shout. 'Tell us, Adam, why changing the house is wrong!'

But Adam said nothing.

Instead, he carried chairs, tables, lamps and chests out to the storage shed behind the kitchen. All afternoon Diana watched him work, repairing broken windows, cleaning floors and moving furniture.

Diana helped move beds, and even Rosie tried to lift and carry until she got bored and wandered away. Mother was wallpapering the baby's room.

At last her dad wiped his sweating forehead. 'I'm afraid I need a rest,' he groaned. 'Diana wanted a small bed and her things moved into Rosie's room. Could you do it by yourselves?'

'Sure we could,' Diana said quickly. It was a chance to talk privately to Adam. She led the way up the stairs.

'I was going to sleep here,' she said as she threw open the door to her old room. 'But it smells kind of bad.'

She watched his face.

Adam froze in the doorway. His eyes darted to the shape of the door to the tower room cut in the wallpaper, and then flicked away again.

'Dad said something must have died in the walls,' Diana went on.

'Died?' Adam's eyes went strangely blank.

'Yes,' Diana stared at him. 'That's why I want to move out of here.'

Adam's eyes flicked to the cuts in the wallpaper again. 'You shouldn't . . .' he choked.

'Shouldn't what?' Diana stared at him.

'Shouldn't be poking around this old house, and changing the f-furniture,' he stammered.

'Why, Adam?' Diana blurted. 'Why can't we change anything in this house?'

But Adam never answered. A sudden cry from downstairs interrupted them.

'Diana! Come and see what I've found.'

Her mother was in the living room, leaning a painting on the shelf above the fireplace. She stepped back, her face glowing with pleasure.

'It was in the sitting room, at the back of a cupboard. 'Look, Diana.'

The painting was the head of a young woman, almost life-size.

She was wearing a deep-blue velvet dress with an old-fashioned lace collar. Her dark hair was pulled back, so you could see how her hairline came to a point, high on her forehead.

Diana's mother stood behind Diana and pulled her hair up and back. 'Isn't it amazing,' she said to Adam, turning Diana's face to show him.

Adam's face was white. His eyes were staring, first at the portrait, then at Diana. 'She looks . . . exactly like you,' he croaked.

Diana's mother laughed again. 'This girl in the picture must have been a Lewis. They have the same eyes, the same smile, the same *widow's peak* in their hair . . .'

'I have . . . to go.' Adam stammered. He gave Diana one last horrified glance and strode from the room.

'Mum!' Diana wanted to scream. 'Why did you have to embarrass me like that!' She jerked away from her mother's hands and shook her hair back down. 'Who cares about my dumb hairline! *Widow's peak,* what a stupid name!'

She ran after Adam, but he was gone.

A night fog was creeping up from the river and the laneway had become a misty white tunnel.

Eight

Adam and his bicycle had disappeared into the fog as though he had never been there.

When she turned around, her father was standing in the driveway. 'I think Adam will be back,' he said. 'He forgot his tools.'

'He won't be back,' Diana kicked the gravel. Her mother had seen to that. The painting of the girl had somehow frightened him. But why? Why did it matter that she looked like some long-lost relative? In some ways, Adam seemed as strange and unreal as everything else around this big old house.

That night, the fog closed in like a thick white glove around the lonely old house on the river. Fingers of fog crept through the crack between the windows while Diana was getting ready for bed.

The damp air made her shiver. Diana banged the stiff old windows shut and latched them in the middle.

The bang woke Rosie. 'Stop making so much noise,' she said sleepily. Rosie was already tucked under the covers on the other side of the big room, with her light out.

'Sorry, Rosiekins. Go back to sleep,' Diana whispered.

She searched under the pillow for her diary. So much had happened since they moved and she hadn't written any of it down. Her diary was her most precious possession. She had been writing in it since she was ten years old.

I want to ask Adam . . . she began. There were so many questions she wanted to ask him. She made a list:

Why is there a secret room in the tower?
Why was it sealed up?
Why can't we move anything in the house?
Why did your grandfather say to be careful?
Why were you so frightened of the picture?
Who is the woman I saw down by the river?

The most important question, Adam couldn't answer, but she wrote it down, anyway:

What did I see in the secret room last night?

Rosie suddenly sat straight up in bed. 'I went down to the river today,' she announced.

'Shh, Rosie, I'm trying to write.'

'I played in the boat house,' Rosie said.

Diana stopped writing. 'You have to be careful playing near the water,' she warned. 'And that old boat house looks like it could cave in any second.'

'You're not my mother!' Rosie snorted. 'Anyway, I can swim. And the old lady was sitting in the boat house, so it must be safe.'

'What old lady?' Diana snapped her diary shut and sat up straight herself.

'I don't know her name. But we had fun.'

'Did she have a black thing over her head?' Diana asked.

'All black,' Rosie agreed. 'Everything on her is black. Even her fingernails are black and her teeth are kind of black.'

'All right.' Diana interrupted. 'What was she doing in the boat house?'

'I already told you. Just sitting.' Rosie said sleepily. 'An old, old lady just sitting in a boat house . . . her shoes were black, her socks were black . . .' Rosie's voice faded out. She was asleep.

So Rosie had seen the woman in black, too! Diana rolled over and gazed at the white patch of foggy window. But what was she doing in that broken-down boat house?

Still wondering, Diana fell asleep.

Hours later, she woke with a jump. Someone was sobbing as if her heart would break.

'Rosie?' Diana called softly. But Rosie was snoring softly in her own bed, not crying.

'Just a bad dream,' Diana told herself, huddling under the covers. She lay there listening to the night noises – a foghorn far away on the river, Rosie's steady breathing.

And then, the sobbing again.

It seemed to be coming from the direction of the window. Diana rolled over and stared at the closed panes of glass. The fog outside shifted and swirled. The window rattled violently, as if someone were trying to break in!

Through it, Diana saw a face – shadowy, drifting, twisted with pain.

For just a moment, it hung in the window, then disappeared. The window rattled again, as if someone was trying to get in.

Diana lay frozen under the covers, feeling once more the chill that had swept over her in the secret room. It started low in her stomach and spread out to her arms and legs, making her feel cold, heavy, powerless to move. She lay there for what seemed like a long time, staring at the fog-shrouded window, listening.

Footsteps pattered past the door, and a long moaning cry came from the hall.

Whatever it was, was now inside.

Diana lay, too frightened to breathe or cry out, clutching the sheet with sweaty palms.

'Rosie?' she finally managed a hoarse whisper.

But there was total silence from the next bed. Rosie was deep in sleep.

'Annnh!' There was another long, moaning wail.

This time, Diana shot out of bed. The crying came from Daniel's room, downstairs. Something was wrong with the baby!

She flew to the door and listened in the dark hall. There was the cry again. She was right! The crying was coming from downstairs. Diana raced down the curved staircase to Daniel's door. It stood open. His window was also flung wide.

Something seemed to be standing over the crib, a shape, hovering low over the sleeping baby.

'Annnh!' he cried again, and the shape gathered itself up and swirled out the window.

Diana rushed to the side of the crib and

switched on the lamp. The baby was lying on his back, his arms outstretched, his eyes closed.

He seemed to be sleeping but his little face was knotted in a worried frown. As Diana watched he rolled his head from side to side and cried out in his sleep again.

'Why doesn't Mum hear him?' Diana asked herself, waiting to hear her mother's footsteps in the hall.

But her mother did not come. A sudden chill breeze reminded her the window was still open. She ran to shut it. Outside, the fog was starting to break up. Diana could see the black points of the cedar trees that grew close to the wall. She stood, staring into the swirling fog, trying to see . . .

Did she imagine it, or was there mocking laughter from out there in the night? Diana grabbed both windows and slammed them shut, then went back to check the baby.

He was sleeping more deeply now. Diana smoothed his soft little forehead till the frown was gone, and he was breathing evenly. There was no need to wake her mother or disturb her father.

Diana climbed wearily back up the stairs to her bed, and slept until morning.

It was a grey morning when she opened

her eyes. Rosie was already up and gone. Breakfast smells drifted up from the kitchen. Diana rolled over and gasped in horror.

There, on the floor lay her precious diary, the pages cut to ribbons.

'The ghost,' cried Louise. 'It cut up her diary. It doesn't want Diana to find the answers to those questions she wrote. It's a warning!'

'I think her little sister Rosie did it,' Charlie said through a mouthful of caramel corn. 'She could have cut the diary up in the morning, while Diana was still asleep.'

'But there is definitely a ghost,' Louise said. 'What did Diana see in the window?'

'The fog. Tree branches. Who knows? Diana seems to have a very good imagination,' Charlie popped another kernel in her mouth and fed one to Ajax.

'And how about the noises? The crying and the footsteps?'

'Maybe there's a rat in the house,' Alex joined in.

'And maybe the noises are just the wind, moaning in the old chimneys. Whho-ooo!' Charlie grinned. 'But I admit, the house is definitely scary. I wouldn't want to be alone there.'

Just then the candle-flames flickered and bent.

'What's that noise?' whispered Louise, clutching Alex's arm.

The four of them went very quiet. Charlie stopped crunching. Alex held her juggling balls still. Jo put her finger to her lips.

Shuffling footsteps were coming towards the dungeon.

Nine

'Who is it?' Louise whispered in terror. 'I thought we were all alone in the house.'

They held their breath, listening to the faint scuffling sounds.

'It's looking for something . . .' Alex whispered. 'Blow out the candles so he doesn't see the light.'

Three faint puffs, and the candles were out.

Now the darkness was total. They squeezed each other's sweaty palms and listened, their hearts pounding.

The sounds had stopped. Whoever was there was listening too. Listening for them.

Then the shuffling began again.

Closer and closer came the little scratchy sounds on the cement floor. The *thing* was almost at the dungeon door. They clutched each other close.

All at once there was a crash and a clatter

68

of something falling. Glass smashing and bottles rolling.

In the next instant they were thrown backwards by the force of something huge and powerful hurling itself at their heads.

There was a storm of fur in their faces. A screech of frightened cat. A slobbery tongue licking in all directions. A strong smell of excited dog.

'AVALANCHE!' Jo screamed.

A hairy mass of St Bernard puppy pounced and whined and licked happily. She managed to pin all four of them down in the darkness.

'How did she find us?' Alex shouted, struggling to sit up.

'She can see in the dark,' Jo puffed. 'She must have got lonely and opened the door to the basement. She's getting too smart!'

'And too big and hairy,' Charlie panted. 'Can't you make her stop rolling on us?'

'Sit, Ava,' Jo commanded. Suddenly they were all free to sit up. They could hear happy panting nearby.

'See, isn't she smart?' Jo said.

'She's brilliant,' Louise laughed. 'But she's drooling all over my lap.'

'What broke out there?' Alex sniffed. 'It smells strong!'

A sweet, powerful scent was wafting through the curtain from the basement. It had replaced the smell of dog.

'Oh no!' Jo groaned. 'Ava must have knocked over my parents' wine rack. I'll have to get a light . . .' She fumbled under the box-table for some matches.

The newly-lighted candle showed broken glass and streams of red wine running in all directions. Charlie and Louise held on to Ava and Ajax, while Jo and Alex cleaned up the mess. The smell of fruit and alcohol hung in the air.

'It smells like we've been drinking,' Charlie giggled. 'How are you going to explain this to your parents?'

'It's not going to be easy,' Jo groaned. 'Ava, why do you do these things?'

Avalanche's tail wagged joyfully and brushed a bowl of pretzels into Louise's lap.

'I'd better put her back upstairs,' Jo sighed. 'Come on, Ava. You're too big and bouncy for the dungeon.'

She left, dragging Avalanche behind her.

'See how easy it is to believe in ghosts, when there is really a simple explanation?' Charlie laughed. 'We all thought Ava was a ghost, or a burglar. We were so scared we were biting our nails!

'I'll bet everything Diana heard and saw has a perfectly normal explanation,' Charlie went on, as she hunted for lost pretzels on her hands and knees.

'I don't think so,' Alex said slowly. 'I think there's more to the story. Am I right, Jo?' she asked, as Jo returned and collapsed on her pile of cushions.

Jo looked around at them. 'Has everybody recovered from being bounced by a St Bernard?'

They nodded. Ajax, the cat, stalked over to Louise on stiff legs and curled up on a corner of the sleeping bag.

'Alex is right. There was more to it.' Jo's voice sank as she looked around at them. Everything in the dungeon was quiet, except for the sound of her voice. Even Avalanche, upstairs, was quiet.

'Go on,' Charlie said breathlessly. 'What happened when Diana saw her diary?'

Jo took a deep breath. 'If you're ready, then I'll tell you what happened,' she began.

Diana pointed to the slashed diary on the floor. She was shaking with anger.

'I didn't cut your book, I didn't, I didn't!' Rosie shouted.

'Then how did it get here, cut to shreds?'

'I don't know.' Rosie's face was red and her blonde curls stood out around it like a golden fuzz.

'Where are those scissors?' Diana demanded angrily.

'What scissors?'

'You know *what* scissors. The silver ones you took from the secret room.'

'You said I didn't have to tell you!' Rosie stood with her hands on her hips. 'You said—'

'That was before you took them and cut up my diary,' Diana stormed. She picked up the cover and tiny fragments of paper fluttered to the floor. 'It's completely ruined.'

'But *I didn't do it*!' Diana could see Rosie was about to throw herself on the floor and scream.

'All right. You didn't do it.' Diana gritted her teeth. 'Just go away and leave me alone.' She knelt down to scoop up the scraps of paper. 'Maybe I can fit some of it back together.'

Rosie was still flushed with anger. 'Mum said to tell you to come quick. She needs you downstairs,' she said, marching to the door.

'Why didn't you tell me?' Diana straightened up quickly.

'You were screaming at me. Remember?' Rosie scooted out the door before Diana could catch her.

Diana threw down the remains of her diary in disgust and raced after her.

Her mother was pacing the dining room with Daniel in her arms. 'Where were you?' she scolded at Diana. 'Have some breakfast quickly and come help with the baby.'

Rosie stuck her tongue out at Diana as she escaped out the door. Somehow, Diana thought bitterly, Mum never considered Rosie old enough to help with Daniel.

If she knew Rosie, she'd be down at the river, poking around the old boat house. Maybe she would meet the old woman again. Diana was impatient to go after her.

But an hour later, there was still no escape in sight. Daniel was fretful and crying. Mum was pacing the floor trying to quiet him.

'Don't you think I should go and check on Rosie?' Diana asked at last. 'She might fall in the river.'

'Yes, dear. I suppose you should,' her mother sighed. 'We told Rosie to stay away from the water, but she doesn't seem to listen much these days.'

Outside it was grey and dull. Heavy dark clouds hung over the river and fog still hid the hills on the other side.

Diana raced down the hill through the ruined rose garden. By now there was a narrow parting of the weeds and brambles where they had run before.

There was no sign of Rosie.

She reached the wide beaten path that ran along the river and looked in both directions. Was that a black shadow, slipping into the old boat house?

Diana tore along the path, jerked open the door and looked inside. The place was dim and shadowy. Black water lapped at the opening in the floor.

Diana shuddered. What an awful place! How could Rosie sit here with the old woman? And where were they now?

She turned and ran from the boat house. Crows were circling the chimneys of the big stone house, calling hoarsely to each other. The house itself was hidden by the screen of weeds and bushes in the overgrown garden.

Where was Rosie? Diana began to be frightened.

She tried to find the path back up to the house, but it was invisible from this side.

There was nothing to do but plunge back into the garden and fight her way through the thorns and clinging vines.

Halfway up the hill she realised she was in a different part of the garden than she had seen before. There was a bit of a clearing in the tangle of weeds, and an old stone fountain in the middle.

A young woman was sitting on the edge of the fountain.

She smiled as Diana came up to her and Diana saw that she was dazzlingly beautiful. Her hair was parted low on one side and swept over her forehead. At the back it was piled in a tumble of curls on top of her head.

She was wearing a soft blue dress and a blue sweater, with a warm scarf around her neck.

'Hello,' the woman said in a clear, low voice. 'You must be Diana.'

'Oh.' Diana stopped suddenly. 'How do you know my name.'

The young woman laughed, a lovely, tinkly laugh. 'I ran into that young man of yours from the hardware store,' she said 'He told me all about you.'

'Adam?' Diana felt herself flushing. 'He's not my . . . young man.'

'He spoke very highly of you,' the young woman shook her head. 'My name is Emma. I live over there,' she pointed through the tangle of brush to the right.

Through the bushes Diana could see the low roof of the gardener's cottage. Emma must be one of the people who rented it for the summer.

'But I thought there was nobody at the cottage now,' she stuttered.

'We come and go,' Emma said. 'The weather seemed nice, so we came.'

'I'm looking for my sister,' Diana said. 'Did you see a little blonde girl come this way?'

'That would be Rosie, right?' The young woman laughed again. 'I told you we had good information. No, I haven't seen her yet. Is she as pretty as you?'

'Much prettier,' Diana said.

'You're going to be a great beauty, wait and see,' Emma smiled. 'I can tell.'

Diana blushed again. 'Have you seen an old woman in a black shawl?' she asked, changing the subject. 'She might know where my sister has gone.'

'You mean Granny Martin?' Emma asked. 'Oh yes, I saw her earlier, walking along the river.'

'Why does she walk across our property all the time?' Diana blurted.

'The path along the water has been there for a long, long, time,' the young woman murmured. 'Much longer than this garden, or the house. For Granny it's a short-cut from her house to the town.'

Diana felt a wave of relief. Granny Martin was a real person. She walked along the path to get to town. There was nothing mysterious about her.

Emma smiled again, and patted the stone rim of the fountain beside her. 'Come and sit with me, and I'll tell you all about this place.'

Diana was dying to, but she shook her head.

'I have to find my sister,' she said. 'We haven't seen her for over an hour, and she doesn't know the estate very well. She might be lost.'

'Oh, I don't think so,' Emma laughed her tinkly laugh. 'Listen to those crows making a fuss. Why don't you see if it's your sister who is bothering them?'

Diana stared at her. What a strange idea!

'They call a bunch of crows a *murder of crows* because they flap around and caw as if someone is being murdered whenever something bothers them,' Emma explained with another laugh. 'It could be Rosie, in this case.'

'I'll go and see. Thank you.' Diana suddenly felt a pang of fear. A murder of crows – it sounded so menacing. 'I hope . . . I'll see you later,' she stammered as she turned to go.

'Oh, I'm sure we'll run into each other.' Emma nodded. 'Be careful now. There's a storm coming.'

The wind whipped Diana's hair in her eyes as she ran towards the house. The storm that had been hanging over the river was coming closer.

Ten

Diana found Rosie sitting up in a pine tree, right where Emma had said she would be. Rosie must have climbed right into a crow's nest. The big black birds still flapped and scolded above her.

'Get down from there!' Diana roared. 'It's dangerous.'

'You're not my—'

'I know I'm not your mother,' Diana shouted. 'But if you don't come down out of that tree, I'm coming up to get you!'

'I double, triple dare you,' Rosie said.

'All right, that's it.' Diana swung her leg up onto the first branch. A few seconds later she was perched beside Rosie, and they were both looking a long way down to the ground.

The wind had begun to sigh in the branches and the trunk swayed beneath them.

'Mum would kill you if she could see

you up this tree,' Diana swallowed hard. She gripped the closest branch and held on tightly.

'No she wouldn't,' Rosie shook her head. 'She doesn't care about me. All she cares about is that stupid smelly baby!'

'Is that why you're being so bad?' Diana asked. 'Because you're mad about Daniel?'

'I don't see what's so great about a baby,' Rosie snuffled. She let go of her branch to wipe her nose and nearly toppled backwards. 'All they do is cry, and spit up, and wet their pants.'

Diana put the arm that wasn't wrapped around the tree around Rosie. 'When I was your age, everybody loved me,' she said.

'Did they?' Rosie looked up at her, and sniffed.

Diana nodded. 'They loved me like crazy until the new baby came along. And then everybody loved her. She was so cute. She had blonde curly hair, and blue eyes.'

'That was me!' Rosie said.

'Right, that was you. I didn't like you much until you were two. Then I discovered you were fun to play with.' Diana gave her a squeeze. 'And you know what the best part was?'

'What?' Rosie had forgotten to cry. 'Was

I really, really cute?'

'Yes. You were. But the best part,' Diana said, 'is that I always got to be the big sister. And you'll always be Daniel's big sister.'

'Then I can tell him to get down out of trees,' Rosie said. 'I'm glad you came to get me. I think I'm stuck. I tried to get down before and I almost fell.'

Diana took a deep breath. 'Climbing up trees is always a lot easier than getting down,' she said. 'You won't fall, just put your feet where I tell you.'

Diana went first. Slowly and carefully, she guided Rosie's feet to each new branch and told her where to put her hands. She kept talking, so Rosie wouldn't think about falling.

The crows screamed at them the whole way down. When they reached the bottom, Rosie gave a huge sigh of relief. 'I did it.'

Their mother appeared in an open window at the side of the house.

'Oh, good. You found her. Come in here, please!'

Their footsteps clattered on the marble floor of the hall.

'Shhh . . .' Their mother came into the hall, looking worried. 'Don't wake the baby. He has a fever – I've finally got him to stop crying and go to sleep. I'm going to lie down,' she went on. 'Can you get yourselves some lunch?'

'Is Daniel very sick?' Rosie asked.

'I don't know, dear. We'll have to watch his fever. Wake me if you hear him cry.'

Diana wondered if she should tell her mother about the shadow she had seen hovering over Daniel's crib the night before. But she knew it would sound like nonsense. And her mother looked too tired and worried to listen to nonsense.

Diana made a peanut butter sandwich for herself and Rosie, but she couldn't eat. She sat and stared at the food on her plate in the big cavernous kitchen.

'Diana, what's wrong?' Rosie said. 'Is it my fault the baby's sick? Did he get sick because I wished he would go away?'

Diana gave her sister a quick hug. 'Of course not. Babies get fevers all the time.'

But Diana felt a cold shiver run down her back. The nightmare returned, of the ghostly figure bending over the baby's crib. Had she dreamed it, or had it been real?

Daniel did not get better that day. By late afternoon his fever was worse and he lay limply in his mother's arms.

Diana and Rosie tiptoed around the great rooms, trying not to make noise.

By seven o'clock, the wind began to shriek and howl around the corners of the old stone house. It roared down the chimneys and rattled the windows. Diana and Rosie sat in the kitchen listening to the fury of the wind.

As darkness fell, the storm hit with full fury. Thunder ripped the air, and lightning flashed through the tall glass windows.

'Poor Dad,' Diana said. 'He must hate the thunder. It sounds like giant cannons, firing all around the house.'

They hadn't seen their father since the storm had started. He was in the den, with the door shut. Their mother was with Daniel in his bedroom. It was as if the house had swallowed everyone up.

'I'm hungry,' Rosie said. 'Isn't anybody going to make dinner?'

A huge crash of thunder seemed to split the air between them. A wail came from the direction of the baby's room. Rosie looked frightened.

'Come on,' Diana said. 'Let's see if we can help.'

Their mother appeared in the kitchen doorway.

'I can't get Daniel to drink anything,' she said. Diana could hear the panic in her voice. 'His fever just keeps going up. I'm going to call the doctor.'

'Isn't it dangerous to use the phone in a thunderstorm?' Diana said. The lightning flashes were coming every few seconds now, and one thunderclap rolled into another.

'I'll have to try . . .' Diana's mother fumbled with the phone book. 'We don't have a doctor. There must be one in Irvington . . .' Irvington was the nearest big town on the river.

Suddenly a fork of lightning seemed to shake the house. They could almost hear the sizzle, and in the same instant the thunder crashed and the lights flickered.

Diana's mother picked up the phone, carefully, and held it to her ear.

'It's dead,' she said. 'The phone is dead. The storm must have knocked out the lines.' Her face was white. 'What are we going to do?'

Diana took a deep breath. 'I'm sure they'll get the phone lines fixed soon,' she said.

'I'll try again to get Daniel to drink something,' her mother hurried from the room. 'I must get his fever down.'

Diana and Rosie followed her. They stood close while their mother tried to get the baby to take a little cool water from his bottle. But Daniel turned his head away. His eyes were closed and the same knot of worry Diana had seen last night creased his hot forehead. She knew at once that he was in danger.

She took a deep breath.

'Mum,' she said gently, 'we have the car. Why don't you drive to the hospital? Dad can go with you and hold Daniel.'

'But what about you and Rosie?' Her mother was already reaching for Daniel's blanket to wrap him up.

'We'll be all right. Rosie and I aren't afraid of storms, are we?' She gripped her little sister's hand tight.

'No-o,' Rosie quavered. 'Diana and I aren't a-afraid.'

'Then I think we'd better go. Please go and get your father,' Diana's mum looked gratefully at her.

As Diana crossed the entrance hall she saw that the rain had started to pour down. It lashed against the windows in full force.

Her father was sitting with his head in his shaking hands.

'The thunder has stopped a bit,' Diana

said. 'Mum wants to take Daniel to the hospital. She can't call the doctor because the phone isn't working. Can you come?'

Her father straightened up and gripped his cane with both hands. His face was a terrible colour, and his voice shook. 'I'll be right there. Help your mother get the baby ready.'

Diana felt tears prickle behind her eyes. Her father was brave – the bravest, but if only he were strong and well right now!

She helped her mother wrap Daniel in two blankets and ran for raincoats and an umbrella. She held Daniel while her parents got the car out and brought it around to the front door.

Outside the rain poured down in a solid wall of water.

'We'll have to go fast, before the lane is completely washed out,' her father shouted over the pounding rain. 'We'll try to stop in town and send someone back to stay with you.'

Diana nodded. It was impossible to make herself heard over the wind and rain. If only they made it to the hospital safely, and in time. She kissed the baby's hot forehead and handed him to her father.

*   *   *

'Oh, poor Diana,' Charlie said. 'She must have been so scared!'

'I would *hate* to be left alone in great big old house,' Louise nodded.

'Listen,' Alex said. 'I think we're going to have our own storm tonight. Listen to that wind.'

Eleven

The wind whistled around the corners of Jo's house and rattled the basement window.

'This is great,' Charlie cried gleefully. 'I hope it's a really big storm. Thunder, lightning, the works!'

'At least we don't have to worry about the lights going out – we have lots of candles,' Jo said. 'Everybody got enough to eat?'

'Let's open the cola and orange pop,' Alex said. 'I ate so many salt and vinegar potato chips while Diana and Rosie were up in that tree, I'm dry as a bone. I don't like heights.'

The bottles of pop were opened and passed around.

'I hope Jason and his friends made it to their sleepover before the storm,' Louise said.

Charlie nodded, opening a chocolate bar and taking a big bite. 'The part of the story that gives me the shivers is the baby being sick,' she said through a mouthful of chocolate. 'I hate to admit it, but I get scared every time Jason gets really sick.'

'I'm almost afraid to hear what happens next,' Alex agreed. 'Just tell us, Jo, is the baby okay?'

Jo smiled a strange, curved-up smile. 'Why don't you let me get back to the story, and tell it in my own way?'

They settled back with fresh supplies of food and drink. Every so often the candle would flicker in the wind through a crack in the window and throw a weird shadow over Jo's face. The other three listened, fascinated, as the story unfolded.

Diana and Rosie stood in the doorway and watched the car lights of Uncle William's car disappear into the wall of rain.

'I hope they make it,' Diana said. 'I hope that Adam fixed that old car so it can go through rain and floods and mud . . .' She thought of Adam's shy smile as he handed the keys to her father, his hand patting the car as if it were a special pet of his.

'Do you think they'll send someone back

to look after us?' Rosie asked, her voice a little shaky.

'It doesn't matter. We'll be fine.' Diana shook herself out of her distant thoughts. She would have to focus on keeping Rosie busy until her parents returned.

'Let's go and see if we can find something to eat,' she said, tugging Rosie inside and shutting the great front door.

They felt small, crossing the high-ceilinged hall, with the lightning flashing around the windows at the top of the stairwell. In the kitchen the light was warmer. Diana heated soup and cut some bread.

'Did you meet Granny Martin today?' Diana asked, as Rosie slurped up her warm soup.

'Who's Granny Martin?' Rosie lifted her tired face.

'That old woman you sat with in the boat house. I met a girl today who knows her. She says Granny takes that old path across the bottom of the garden to get to town.'

Rosie shook her head. 'No, I didn't see her.'

'What did you talk about, yesterday?' Diana asked.

'Oh, just old stuff,' Rosie shrugged. 'What the house was like before it got all wrecked, and how the garden was so beautiful, with roses and marigolds, and stuff like that.'

'It must have been nice, once upon a time,' Diana agreed.

Thunder cracked again, close to the house, and made them jump.

'Diana!' Rosie screamed.

'It's okay,' Diana soothed. 'The storm must be almost over now. I'll bet that was the last really loud clap of thunder.'

But she was wrong. The storm seemed to be getting worse. The wind howled through the trees around the house and shrieked down the chimneys. The sound of the rain on the roof was deafening.

'Diana,' Rosie said. 'The roof is leaking. Look.'

She pointed upwards.

Diana choked back a scream. Water was coming through the kitchen ceiling above them. They jumped up to avoid getting splashed by the drips hitting the table. The drips came from a wet patch, in the shape of a bird with outstretched wings. It suddenly reminded Diana of something she had seen recently. The crows – circling over the house.

Diana recognised the wet patch. It was the same stain Adam had been so frightened to see. The same dark stain that was on the floor of the secret room, right over their heads.

'Let's go up to our room,' Diana said shakily. 'Then, if the storm gets worse, we can snuggle in our beds.'

Rosie nodded miserably.

Diana quickly searched the kitchen drawers. She was looking for candles and matches. If this kept up, the power would fail, just like the telephone. The thought of being upstairs in the dark, alone, was more than she could bear!

'There!' she managed a smile. 'I've got emergency candles. You bring emergency cookies. We'll sit out the storm like brave adventurers.'

'Like travellers to a strange land,' Rosie joined in the game. She got a box of cookies and followed Diana up the kitchen stairs to the second floor.

Once in their room, Diana set everything down on her bedside table and pulled the lamp close.

'I think I'm going to try to put the pages of my diary back together,' she said cheerfully.

'Oh,' said Rosie.

'You don't have to worry. I'm not mad any more.'

'That's good,' Rosie said. 'Because I didn't cut it, you know. I told you that.'

'I know,' Diana said. She brought the scraps of paper and the empty cover of the diary over to the table. It was not worth getting in a fight with Rosie again, but of course she must have done it. There was no one else.

'When I'm finished, we'll play a game,' she told Rosie. 'We'll each get one point for every clap of thunder we hear.'

'Then who will win?' Rosie asked.

'The person who hears the last clap,' Diana said.

Picking up a scrap from her diary, Diana saw, for the first time, that the paper had been folded into a tiny square. Puzzled, she smoothed it out.

No! Diana's heart lurched.

She smoothed out another scrap, and another.

'No!' she wanted to scream. She covered the scraps with shaking hands. Rosie mustn't see. Each one was in the shape of a bird with outstretched wings. Like the stain in the ceiling, each one was cut in the shape of a crow.

The work had been done by thin, very sharp scissors. But this was not the work of an eight-year-old. Rosie still cut the arms and ears off her paper dolls. These birds were perfect, each feather exact.

If Rosie had not cut up her diary, who had? Diana's brain was whirling.

At that second, CRACK! Thunder split the night and the lights went out.

Diana clutched Rosie close to her in the darkness.

'You're shiv-shivering,' Rosie said in a small voice.

'It just surprised me, that's all,' Diana croaked. Who had cut the pages of her diary into the shapes of crows?

'Let me light the candles,' she said, trying to keep her voice steady. The flickering candles soon burned brightly, their flames high.

'There's too much wind,' Diana said. 'The candles will burn down too fast.' They must not lose the candlelight.

She forced herself to walk across the floor and reach out into the night to grab the banging windows and fasten them tightly. The rain-whipped branches caught at her nightgown, making her gasp, soaking the sleeves.

'Do I get a point for the big boom that turned off the lights?' Rosie asked.

'Two points,' Diana said. 'That was the loudest thunderclap yet.'

Rosie smiled. 'I like this game.'

'Maybe we can play it in bed,' Diana tried to keep the quaver out of her voice. 'That way, we can keep warm, and still keep score.'

'You wouldn't be trying to get me to go to sleep, would you?' Rosie asked. 'Because I won't until the thunder is done.'

'I'm just a bit cold,' Diana said. 'Here, let me tuck you in, and I'll put a candle on the table beside you.'

She settled Rosie in bed, lit her candle and then climbed, still shivering, under her own covers.

'One point for you,' Rosie chanted as the thunder rolled on, 'and one for me. I win!' she said sleepily. 'I think that was the end.'

Diana lay still and quiet until Rosie's breathing became deep and regular. The ceiling and walls seemed to close in upon her, and then become huge, so that she felt like a tiny speck in a tiny bed in a massive room.

All at once she heard distant knocking. There was a large brass knocker on the front door that echoed through the house.

Diana froze in her bed. She was not going to get up and walk the dark hallways and the dark stairs. She could not.

The knocking came again. BOOM! BOOM!

'I can't,' Diana whispered into the darkness.

But what if it were someone sent by her parents to help? She *must* answer the door.

Twelve

Diana paused at the top of the long flight of stairs.

'Boom, boom, boom!' The sound of the door knocker echoed through the empty front hall.

Step by step, clutching her candle, Diana moved downward. At the bottom, she halted again. Had the knocking stopped?

'Boom, boom, boom!' There it was again. Her image wavered in the mirror opposite the staircase, ghostly in the candlelight.

She took a deep breath, and started across the hall.

'Who's there?' she called, as she reached the door.

'It's Emma. Let me in,' came a voice from outside.

Emma! Brimming with relief, Diana reached for the door lock. Emma had come to help.

As she opened the door, a gust of wind seemed to blow Emma into the hall. She was wearing a long coat and a scarf over her head.

'I'm so glad to see you!' Diana cried. She could have hugged the young woman. 'Did my parents stop at the cottage on the way to the hospital? How did they know you were there?'

'I suppose they saw our lights . . . our candle lights,' Emma smiled. 'Your lights are out too, I see.'

As if to warn them that the storm was not over, a bright flash of lightning flashed around the entrance hall, and in the vivid light, Diana saw that Emma's clothes were dripping wet.

'Oh, you're soaked!' Diana cried. 'I'm sorry it took me so long to answer the door. I – I was upstairs with Rosie. I think she's asleep.'

She remembered her manners. 'Let me take your coat.'

Emma stepped back. 'It's all right, she said. 'It will dry. Why don't we go in the kitchen, where it's warmer.'

Diana thought of the stain, dripping, in the ceiling of the room. But it's just a leak in the roof, she told herself. With Emma here, I won't be afraid.

She led the way to the kitchen, and set the candle on the table. It was warmer in here, and she collapsed gratefully into an armchair near the stove.

Emma sat on the other side of the table, her face in shadow.

'Where did you say your sister was?' she asked.

'She's upstairs, asleep, I hope,' Diana murmured. Diana felt powerfully sleepy herself. She had not slept well for two nights, and the stress of the day had worn her out. Still, she thought, it's probably not very polite to go to bed when Emma has just arrived.

Emma seemed to read her thoughts. 'Why don't you stay here and keep warm, while I go and check on your little sister.'

'That's very nice of you,' Diana stifled a yawn. 'Our room is the last one on the right, at the end of the hall.'

Emma padded softly from the room.

Diana watched the flickering candle flame. Her eyes were closing in spite of herself. She would soon be fast asleep in the chair. She forced herself to blink. There was something she should think about . . .

Suddenly, she knew what it was. Emma had no candle. She was going upstairs, trying to find Rosie's room in the dark!

Diana shot out of her chair, seized the candle and hurried to the stairs. The rain was drumming on the roof – there was no use calling. All was dark and silent above.

Diana ran up the carpeted steps and down the hall. There was no sign of Emma – somehow she must have made her way in the darkness.

She flung open the door of their room, and gasped, 'Emma!'

Emma was bending over Rosie's bed, in the same way that some evil thing had hovered over the baby the night before. The candle on the bedside table lit her long dark hair, flowing loose around her face.

She turned suddenly at Rosie's gasp.

Diana froze in fear. Emma's beautiful face was twisted into an evil stare. Her hair was thrown back to reveal the point in the centre of her forehead. It was the face of the girl in the painting with the *widow's peak*.

'Get away from my sister!' Diana rushed forward.

The figure seemed to swirl in the air. It floated towards Diana without touching the floor, arms outstretched like a bird of prey.

'You have taken something that belongs to *me*!' The voice was terrible, deep and low. '*He* gave them to me. I will have them back!'

Diana turned and ran. She could feel Emma behind her, catching up with her. Sobbing for breath, Diana hurtled down the narrow kitchen stairs. She heard a hoarse cry, '*I will have them back.*'

She dashed across the kitchen to the door. As she reached for the doorknob, she turned and saw outstretched arms in the darkness, a pale shape with flowing hair.

The door was locked.

Helplessly. Diana yanked at the door-knob. 'Open, oh please open!' she begged.

In the dungeon, they sat stunned into silence as Jo stopped to take a drink. The only sound was the wind, battering the world above the basement.

'Whew!' Charlie let out her breath. '*Emma* is the ghost! I thought the whole thing was just in her imagination.' She was sitting close to Louise, and popping pretzels nervously into her mouth one after the other.

'Why didn't Diana recognise Emma in the rose garden?' Alex shivered. 'I mean, she had seen the portrait.'

'Paintings don't always look like people in real life,' Louise said. 'Anyway, her hair was down over her forehead. That would make her look different.'

At that moment, a flash of light lit the window above them.

'It seems like our thunderstorm is about to start,' Alex said.

'I don't hear any thunder,' Charlie said.

'It's still too far away,' Alex nodded, 'but it's coming closer.'

Thirteen

'Come on, Jo, you can't stop now. Tell us if Diana got out safely,' Alex begged.

'What's the difference?' Charlie said. 'Ghosts can walk through walls. Even if Diana slams the door in her face, she still isn't safe.'

'My thumbs are pricking.' Louise shivered. 'Go on, Jo.'

So Jo did. She crouched low, by the table, and let her voice rise to Diana's desperate scream . . .

'Open, oh please open!'

She felt cold fingers slip around her neck.

Frantically, she tried the lock again. This time the knob turned. Diana flung the door open and rushed . . . straight into the arms of a short figure dressed entirely in black.

Behind her, Diana thought she heard a ghostly moan. The fingers slid from her throat, down her back, leaving a trail of shivers.

'Here, child. What's the matter?' The figure folded down a huge black umbrella. Diana looked into an ancient, wrinkled face.

'It's just Granny Martin, child. Don't be afraid. Come inside now. We're getting wet.'

Diana obeyed. She was too shocked and frightened to do anything else. Her legs felt like rubber.

Granny Martin stood her dripping umbrella beside the door, and took off her shawl. Under it, her grey hair was wound into a tight bun.

'You do look done in,' she clucked. 'What's been frightening you?'

Diana looked wildly around the kitchen. The candle still threw its pool of light on the table. But the rest of the room was deep in shadow.

'There was someone . . . something . . . here,' she stammered. 'My parents are out. The baby is sick.'

'Did this strange person have a name by any chance?' Granny tipped her head to one side and smiled.

'She said her name was Emma,' Diana whispered.

Granny Martin shook her head. 'I thought so. When they said you looked just like all the other Lewis girls, I worried she might come back. And then, you've been *disturbing* things, haven't you?'

'My little sister told you,' Diana said.

'That's right dear. She's a lovely child, but not at all like a Lewis. Not at all like Emma.'

'Who is she?'

'*Was*, dear, *was*. She's been gone for fifty years or more.' Granny threw Diana a kind look. 'You've had a bad shock, dear. Let me fix you a warm drink and then we'll talk.'

She moved around the kitchen as though she knew exactly where everything was. As though she lived there.

Diana collapsed thankfully in the armchair by the stove. 'How do you know about Emma?' she asked.

'I was here. I saw the whole thing,' Granny nodded. 'Oh, yes, I was here.' She put a pot of milk on the stove, mixed cocoa and sugar in a cup and added it to the milk.

'It all happened right here in this house . . .' She looked up at the stain in the ceiling.

'Right up there, in that tower room. They never could fix that leaky roof. It always comes through.'

The old woman stirred the cocoa. 'The truth is, nobody has been able to live in this house since it happened. Your Great-uncle William tried, but he couldn't stay. Couldn't sleep.'

She handed Diana a steaming cup of hot chocolate. 'But I'm getting ahead of myself. You drink this. Then we'll talk.'

But Diana's mind was racing too fast to relax. 'Emma is a ghost?' she asked.

'I don't know what you've seen,' the old woman nodded, 'or who you've met. But *my* Emma was a beautiful young girl, the gardener's daughter on this estate. She fell in love with the gentleman of the house. They used to meet, every night, at the boat house.'

The hot chocolate was going straight to Diana's toes, warming her whole body.

'Did he love her?'

'He said he did, and promised to marry her, too. He bought her presents – lovely dresses and fine jewels. And he made a beautiful room for her, up above this kitchen, furnished with silk, and silver, and lace . . .'

'I know,' Diana said. 'I've seen it.'

Granny shook her head. 'Oh dear,' she said. 'Then it's no wonder she's unhappy. You've been in her special room.'

'What happened?' Diana demanded.

'The room was ready for the bride,' Granny went on, 'and she used to come and visit, and try on her wedding dress and jewels. And then he went away to New York City and married someone else.'

'Why?'

'No one knows for certain. It might have been he never meant to marry Emma. Or it might have been his grandmother. She controlled the family money, and they all danced to her tune.'

'And then what happened?'

'It was terrible for Emma. The night before he returned with his wife she locked herself in her beautiful room and stabbed herself with a long pair of silver scissors he had given her. He found her dressed in her wedding gown, lying in a pool of blood. Up there.' She pointed at the stain.

'She left him a note, pinned on his pillow, to meet her at the boat house.'

Diana nodded. She had seen that note.

'He went to the boat house, mad with grief. But it was not the live girl he met, so

107

they say. Whatever happened, he was never in his right mind again.'

Granny sighed, and closed her eyes. 'He and his wife moved away, and the house was closed. Nothing lives here now, but the crows in the chimney.'

'How do you know all this?' Diana found herself shivering. She could picture the terrible meeting in the boat house.

'I was a maid in this house. I loved them both, him and her,' Granny said sadly. 'They were so beautiful together.'

'That's why you sit in the boat house,' Diana said.

'I keep my eye on things. I have been able to control her, up until tonight.' Granny's old eyes looked straight into Diana's. 'You must not disturb her room. She can't rest when things are touched by other hands.'

Rosie had snapped the scissors as though they were a toy, Diana thought with a shudder. The same scissors Emma had used to end her life!

'My sister,' she said with a gasp. 'I have to go and see if she's all right.'

'I'll come with you, dear,' Granny Martin said.

Granny took the candle and led the way

to the front hall. Diana stumbled to keep up. Her legs still felt weak and wobbly.

'Those stairs look rather steep,' Granny said. 'My heart is a little weak. I think I will leave you here, child.'

And then, as they reached the bottom of the stairs, Diana saw something that almost made her legs collapse. The candlelight glowed in the large, framed mirror, but there was no reflection of Granny's face!

The lines from an old poem burst into her head:

> *No shadow on the new-mown grass*
> *No mirror image as you pass*

A ghost! Granny was a ghost too.

'Thank you' Diana managed to stammer. 'Thank you for the cocoa.'

'I was glad to help,' the old woman sighed and handed the candle to Diana. She felt the cold brush of Granny's fingers on her own.

'Don't forget,' Granny said, as she faded into the blackness of the hall. 'Put everything back, exactly where it was.'

Diana turned and fled up the stairs.

In their room, Rosie was sleeping restlessly. Her eyelids twitched, and her cheeks were flushed.

Diana shook her by the shoulder. 'Rosie. Rosemary. Wake up!'

Rosie blinked and sat up.

'What's the matter? Oh, Diana, I was having an awful dream!'

'Never mind. You have to tell me where you hid the scissors. I know I promised, but I have to find them. I have to put them back. It might save Daniel's life!'

Please let Rosie believe me, she prayed silently. It might save her life, too!

'They're under my socks, in my drawer,' Rosie sighed.

Diana hurried across the room and threw open the drawer. The silver scissors seemed to burn in her hand as she reached for them.

'Are you going back in that smelly secret room?' Rosie asked. Her eyes were huge.

'Yes. Now,' Diana nodded. 'And I want you to stay right here in your bed,' she commanded. 'Don't move, until I come back.'

Jo shivered as another flash of light travelled across the window, throwing shadows into the dungeon.

'Poor Emma,' Alex said. 'Imagine how she must have felt. Betrayed. Is that the word, Jo?'

Jo nodded.

'But the thing is,' Charlie said, 'she

didn't wait for him to explain *why* he married someone else. Maybe his grandmother tricked him into it. Maybe he still loved Emma.'

'She should have waited to find out,' Louise agreed.

'Her heart was broken,' Alex shook her head. 'What difference did it make?'

Fourteen

'Is it freezing in here, or is it just me?' Louise shivered, pulling another blanket around her shoulders.

They were all huddling close together, close to the light and Jo's voice. Louise had squeezed Ajax so tight she wriggled out of her hands and fled into the shadows of the dungeon.

'I think it's just this story,' Charlie hugged herself. 'Whew! It's giving me goosebumps! I wish Diana would just hurry up and put the scissors back.'

'I don't think she should even try to go into that secret room again,' Louise cried. 'She should get Rosie up, and get out of that house, now!'

'I still suspect Adam,' Charlie said. 'Where is he when all this is happening?'

Jo shook her head. 'All Diana knew was that she had to undo the damage she and

Rosie had done. Granny had said: *She can't rest when things are disturbed.* Everything must be the same in the room as the day Emma died. Diana had to make it the same – then they would be safe.'

Jo looked around at her three friends. They huddled even closer, listening as Jo's voice sank almost to a whisper.

Diana turned the delicate silver scissors in her hand. In the candle glow she could see the initials E. L. engraved on the long sharp blades. E for Emma. L for Lewis.

'Diana, will you be all right?' Rosie tugged at her sleeve.

'Yes, Rosie, I promise I'll be fine.' Diana tried to sound as definite as she possibly could. 'But whatever you hear, and whatever you see, I want you to stay right here.'

'Okay,' Rosie promised in a weak voice. 'But please hurry back. I'll be scared.'

Diana gripped the candle in one hand and the scissors in the other.

Her footsteps creaked down the long hall.

As she got nearer to the branching hallway a chill draught wrapped around her ankles. A breath of clammy air fluttered the candle.

Diana stopped, and waited for the flame

to burn stronger. The candle must not go out!

She held the silver scissors out in front of her like a sword. The blades gleamed in the candle glow.

One step. Then another. She had reached the large bedroom at the end of the hall. She saw the jagged outline of the door, cut in the wallpaper on the far wall.

Beyond that door lay the stairs to the secret room.

Diana paused, gathering her courage. Her head felt hot and dizzy, despite the strange chill in the air.

The sharp smell of bats made her stomach churn. Shadows gathered themselves around her. What waited for her on the other side of the hidden door?

Diana set the candle carefully on the floor. She reached for the hole in the wallpaper where the doorknob should be.

Once more, she tugged and pulled, but the old layer of paper, jammed in the crack, held the door tightly shut.

From somewhere above came a low moan.

A chill that made her teeth chatter swept over Diana.

'I will get in,' she vowed.

She wrenched at the door.

It flew open suddenly, throwing her backwards.

Diana staggered, protecting the candle flame. The stairs beyond the door were dark and waiting. Diana forced herself to climb the narrow, winding steps. At the top, she paused.

In the dim candle glow, Diana could see the dressing table with its silver tray, Over there, on that tray, that's where she must place the scissors.

She took a step forward and froze. The room seemed filled with hate and anger. Diana could feel it piercing her, pinning her feet to the floor.

'Emma Lewis!' she cried out. 'This is your great-great-cousin, Diana. I've come to put things back the way they were.' She held out the silver scissors.

At that moment a furious blast of air snuffed out the candle. Diana gasped in the darkness.

But it was not quite dark. Over there, by the dressing table, was a thin blue light.

Diana felt its coldness, its despair. The light began to move, floating from side to side like someone swaying in sorrow. Then it seemed to grow larger and larger, filling the room.

Diana's heart thudded in her chest. The light was moving towards her, looming over her . . .

'Stop!' she screamed. She hurled the silver scissors with all her strength, right at the centre of the cold blue light.

There was a ghastly groan. The blue light quivered and shrank for a moment. In the dressing table mirror, Diana seemed to see the shape of a woman, clutching her heart.

Then the pale light swirled into a coil of fury. It rushed at Diana. She flung out her arms, blocking the doorway, thinking of Rosie, helpless in her bed.

'NO!' she shouted.

The blue light spun high into the air and aimed itself at Diana in one concentrated beam.

She felt it pass like a freezing shudder, straight through her. The floor rushed up to meet her and everything swirled into blackness.

Meanwhile, Rosie waited anxiously for Diana to return. Her candle burned steadily beside the bed. The storm outside had stopped pounding the house and for a moment there was an eerie silence.

And then Rosie heard footsteps coming

up the stairs. She hugged her quilt tight to her chin with clenched fists.

It wasn't Diana, the footsteps were too heavy.

It wasn't father. He couldn't climb stairs.

Then who was coming slowly towards her room? Rosie was too frightened to call out.

The footsteps creaked in the hall outside. Rosie caught her breath and choked back a scream.

Closer and closer came the slow, steady steps. They paused, as if listening for something. Rosie did not dare to breathe.

Creak, creak, creak. They started up again. Rosie pulled the quilt up over her head. Maybe whoever it was would not see her.

The footsteps stopped at her doorway. She could hear the door squeak on its hinges. Rosie held her breath until she thought her lungs would burst.

Then she heard a horrified cry. 'Diana! Are you all right?' Rosie threw back the quilt and sucked in a big breath.

'Adam, it's me. I'm hiding. I thought you were a ghost!'

'Rosie!' Adam held a light up to look at her. 'You gave me such a scare,' his voice was shaking. 'I saw a body in the bed, with its head covered. Where's Diana?'

'She went . . .' Rosie started to explain. A sudden terrible scream from the dark regions of the house cut her short.

'NO-*o-o-o*!'

Adam and Rosie stared at each other.

'That's Diana!' Rosie said, leaping out of bed. 'She went to put the scissors back in the secret room. Come on!'

She grabbed Adam's hand and together they raced towards the sound of the scream.

The next thing Diana knew, a yellow light was shining in her eyes. Rosie and Adam were bending over her. Emma's ghost *passed right through me*, she thought fuzzily. *But I'm still alive.*

'What happened?' Adam sounded worried.

'Adam! What are you doing here?' Diana sat up carefully. She was still shivering so hard her teeth were chattering.

'Your parents sent a message . . . I came on my bike,' Adam stammered, and Diana saw that the yellow glow came from a bike lamp in his hand.

'They think your baby brother is going to be okay,' Adam said. 'but he has to stay in the hospital. He still has a high fever.'

Rosie squeezed Diana's hand. 'Did you . . . put the scissors back?'

Diana shook her aching head. There was danger all around them. 'We have to get out of here,' she moaned. 'Out of this room, and out of this house.'

Adam lit the way down the main stairs, through the dark hall and out the front door. Rosie clutched Diana's arm in both her hands.

The night greeted them with a blast of wind and rain.

'We can't stay out here,' Adam cried. He turned to go back inside.

'No!' Diana screamed. Behind her, the house's face was blank and horrible. She would not go back in there!

A sudden bolt of lightning blazed before them. There was an instant CRACK! of thunder and a cracking, tearing sound. The pine tree that Rosie had climbed that afternoon split in two and crashed to the ground.

Rosie shrieked with terror. 'The lightning is going to hit us. It's going to hit us!'

'The boat house!' Diana shouted over the howl of the wind. 'We'll be safe there.'

She led the way, racing through the rain-soaked garden, down to the river. Adam's light bobbed on the swollen waters.

The waves dashed against the shore, wetting their feet as they hurried along the path. Moments later, the boat house loomed out of the darkness. The flooded river hurled itself at the old plank walls, and the boat house leaned even closer to the dark water.

Diana seized the door handle and the door blew out of her hand, slamming against the wall. 'Hurry,' she yelled. 'Before we get blown away.'

Inside the boat house, the water slurped and sucked below the wooden floor. But at least they were out of the storm. Dripping wet and shivering with the cold, they stared at the black square of deep water where once boats had floated.

'Be careful,' Adam pulled Rosie back from the edge of the hole. 'The water is very high. Don't get too close.'

Diana looked up, into the shadows of the open rafters. Her head spun. Was there something up there, something faintly blue, and pulsing?

All at once they were surrounded by a wrenching, tearing sound.

'Adam?' Diana screamed, over the noise of the wind and water. 'What's that noise?'

The boat house was groaning, like a thing in pain.

'It's coming apart!' Adam shouted. 'Quick, get out! The boat house is collapsing!'

Now they could feel the floor shifting under their feet. With a terrible scream, Rosie slid towards the open water. Diana reached out for her, but the boat house gave a sudden lurch and Rosie was gone.

Diana flung herself on the floor. All was black below her. The huge old timbers pounded into the mud at the bottom of the river groaned as they tore loose.

'Rosie!' Diana screamed. 'Where are you?'

'It's too late,' Adam said. 'She'll be washed out into the river!'

The boat house was breaking up all around them. The floor was now on a terrible slant. 'I can't let her go!' Diana cried. 'Help me, Adam.'

'I can't swim,' Adam moaned. He reached for a rope over a beam. 'Here. Tie this around your waist. I'll hold the other end as long as I can.'

Diana fumbled with the heavy rope, tying it in a firm knot. She kicked off her shoes and plunged head-first into the dark hole in the floor.

When she came up, all was blackness. 'Rosie!' she screamed, gulping down a mouthful of water. It was madness under the boat house. The water was churned to fury by the storm. Waves pounded the sides and sucked water in and out through the open beams.

How would she ever find Rosie in this whirling mass of black water?

She trod water furiously, trying to see.

Suddenly, a pale blue light flickered in front of her eyes.

'Emma!' Diana took a ragged breath.

The light spun into a dark corner.

Diana followed it with her eyes. There was something white there, something caught in a V between two beams.

'Rosie!' Diana screamed again.

Rosie was caught in the fork of the wood. Diana swam towards her. The blue light wavered and pulled away.

Diana yanked and tugged at her sister's body until at last it floated free.

'Oh, Diana,' Rosie flung her arms around Diana's neck. 'I was stuck.'

Gasping for breath, Diana broke Rosie's stranglehold on her throat and swam towards the edge of the hole, lifting Rosie's pale face high.

'Adam,' she choked. 'I've got her. Hurry. Pull us up!'

The whole boat house was in motion. A

beam crashed into the water centimetres from her head. But Adam was there, hauling them in, hand over hand, lifting Rosie's limp body to the narrow walkway.

'It's breaking up!' he screamed. 'We'll have to jump for it.'

The floor gave a final lurch under Diana's feet. She clasped Rosie's arm tight and held on while Adam tugged them toward the door.

The blue light hovered over them.

Diana gasped in horror. Between the open door and the shore was a space of racing black water. The boat house was being swept away.

'JUMP!' Adam screamed and together, holding hands, they leaped for the bank.

Diana landed half in the water. She felt it pulling her under, but her hands were firmly gripped in Adam's and she was yanked up beside him.

They stood gasping for air, soaked to the skin, their hair plastered to their foreheads.

The blue light swayed in the boat house doorway.

'It's the ghost,' Diana cried. 'It's Emma!'

At that moment, the boat house gave a shudder. With a last wrenching groan, it sank sideways into the dark water and was swept away. The blue light flickered over the river and then was sucked down into the vortex.

Diana clutched Rosie's shivering body close. 'She's gone,' Diana whispered.

There was a moment of silence as the three of them gazed at the place where the boat house had disappeared. The storm-tossed river rolled on, leaving no trace.

Adam nodded. 'Gone for ever, this time. They say ghosts can't cross the open water.' He grabbed Diana's hand. 'You're both freezing,' he said. 'We should go back to the house.'

Diana was shuddering from head to toe. 'I don't know if Emma was trying to drown us or save us,' she stammered, 'but I never would have found Rosie in time without her. I hope she has some peace, now that the boat house is destroyed.'

She took a deep breath. Emma's ghost had tried to destroy her, back there in the secret room. But she had been too strong. The storm had tried to drown them, but they had survived. She suddenly knew that she would remember this night all her life, and be strong enough to face whatever came her way.

Fifteen

The rain had finally stopped, and the wind died as Rosie, Adam and Diana staggered up to the house through the wet garden.

Diana paused at the front door. She looked up at the tower and peaked roofs of the old house and shivered. 'I don't want to go in yet,' she said.

Adam went inside to find blankets to wrap around Diana and Rosie. The three of them huddled on the front steps in the warm damp night. The moon had come out and crickets started to sing.

'Now, tell me about the ghost,' Rosie demanded.

'I can't right now,' Diana murmured. All at once she was too tired to talk. 'You tell, Adam.'

Adam's face was pale in the moonlight. 'I've been hearing about this house all my life,' he said. 'My grandfather told me

125

stories about the girl that died upstairs. They say she haunts this house.'

'Yes,' Diana said. 'I saw her in the secret room, the night Rosie took her scissors. And I saw her again right down there in the garden. I thought she was alive. She was so beautiful . . .'

She looked up at Adam. 'You must have been frightened to ride out here tonight by yourself,' she said.

Adam nodded. Diana thought she could see a ghost of a smile on his lips. 'I was pretty scared,' he admitted. 'But there was no one else to come. I had to bring your father's message.'

'I'm glad you came,' Diana sighed. 'It was brave.'

'Forget how brave he was. Who was the ghost?' Rosie insisted.

'Her name was Emma,' Diana said. 'Granny Martin knew her.' Diana clutched her blanket closer. 'I think Granny is a ghost, too.'

Adam gave a start. 'What makes you think that?'

Diana stared up at his serious face. 'Granny was here tonight. She walked all this way through the storm. *Then* she said her heart was too weak to climb the stairs. And when she stood in front of the mirror you couldn't see her reflection.'

Adam shook his head. 'Granny can't be a ghost!' he said. 'She's a little strange, and she's very old, but she's real. I see her in the store almost every day.'

'Come inside, and I'll show you.'

Diana led the way across the hall to the mirror at the foot of the stairs.

'Granny was standing right here,' Diana said, pulling Adam in front of the mirror.

'Hold the light,' Adam said. 'Shine it on the mirror.'

In the beam from Adam's bike lamp, his image came and went in the glass.

Diana gave a gasp. One moment Adam was there, the next, he was gone.

'I thought so,' Adam laughed. 'It's an old mirror. The silvering is wearing off the back. See, I disappear if I move this way.'

Diana sighed with relief. It was just an old mirror. 'Come on, Rosie,' she said. 'Let's get some dry clothes.'

'I'm glad Granny's not a ghost,' Rosie said, as they clattered down the stairs a few minutes later. 'But what about the girl that died upstairs? Who was she?'

'Her name was Emma Lewis,' Adam said. 'You have a picture of her over the fireplace.'

He pointed to the living room. 'It scared the life out of me, the first time I saw it.'

They crossed the hall to the living room. Adam shone his lamp on the portrait of Emma. She looked sad and lonely in the pale yellow light.

'You looked just like her when your mother pulled your hair back,' Adam grinned shyly at Diana. 'But now that I know you, I don't think you look the same at all.'

Even in the lamplight, Diana could see him blush.

'Poor Emma,' Diana sighed. 'What a sad life she had. No wonder she couldn't let go of that secret room or her belongings. It was the one place she had been happy.'

'Well, she didn't have to be so picky about her old scissors,' Rosie pouted.

At that moment they heard the crunch of tyres on the gravel outside the house. Headlights shone through the living room window.

'Someone's here!' Rosie cried.

They ran to the kitchen door, Adam lighting the way.

It was Diana's father, come to take them to Irvington. He had found a hotel room close to the hospital, where they could spend the night.

'The baby had a close call,' he told them. 'The doctors say we might have to take him to the hospital in the city tomorrow.' He hugged his daughters close with both arms.

'How about you kids?' he asked. 'Has everything been all right?'

Diana looked at Rosie and they both looked at Adam. He shrugged.

'Just fine, Dad,' Diana said. 'It's been a pretty quiet night.'

Her father smiled. 'That's good. You'd better go upstairs and pack as much as you can,' he said. 'We might not be back here for a while.'

Diana climbed the curved staircase and creaked down the dark hall one last time, Rosie trotting behind her.

Rosie chattered as Diana pulled things out of drawers and spread them on the bed. 'I sure would like to take those scissors,' she sighed.

'Don't even think of it!' Diana said sharply. 'We are not going back in that secret room for anything – especially not the scissors!'

As she threw her clothes in her old brown suitcase, Diana suddenly knew she would never see the secret room again. They would never be back in this house.

She sat beside Adam on the drive to town. Diana was dizzy with fever, but happy to be close to Adam.

They stopped in town to let him out. He squeezed her hand to say goodbye.

'Thank you for everything,' Diana's father called. 'We'll be seeing you, Adam.'

'Will we?' Diana wondered, as Adam walked away in the darkness. 'Will we ever see him again?'

'Oh, don't you dare stop there,' Charlie cried. 'What happened next? Did she ever see Adam again?'

'There isn't much more to tell,' Jo began.

'Just a minute,' Alex held up her hand. 'Look up there.'

They all stared up at the small dungeon window. The same light they had seen before was flashing back and forth.

Alex stood up, hands on her hips. 'I'm starting to think that it can't be lightning,' she declared.

'Don't you dare say it's anything spooky, Alex.' Louise gripped Jo's arm. 'We're safe down here, right, Jo?'

'Perfectly safe, as long as the light isn't *blue*.' Charlie laughed a spooky laugh.

Sixteen

'I think there's somebody else out there,' Alex said.

'It's just cars going past,' Charlie scoffed. 'Look, I can show you how the mirror in the story worked.'

Charlie held up a two-sided mirror in a frame. 'If you take it apart, you'll find there's a layer of silvery stuff inside,' she explained. 'That's what gives you the reflection.'

Charlie took apart the frame to show them.

'That's wonderful,' Jo clapped. 'I suppose you think there wasn't a real ghost in Aunt Diana's house at all!'

'I'm suspicious of Adam,' Charlie said. 'After all, his family wanted to buy the old place. And Adam had keys to the car. He might have had keys to the house, too. He could have rigged things up to look spooky, just to scare Diana's family away.'

Just then, there was another flash of light at the window.

A sharp knock on the glass made them almost jump out of their skins!

'What's that?'

'Look!'

It was Mick's face at the window. He pointed at Alex and mouthed the words, 'I want to talk to you!'

'He's no ghost!' Charlie said.

'But he will be, when we get our hands on him,' Jo said. 'What do you want to do, Alex?'

Alex had hidden her head in her hands. Suddenly she straightened up and reached for a piece of paper and a marker. She scribbled a note and held it up to the window for Mick to read.

What do you want?

'I'm sorry,' Mick called through the window. Alex flipped her sign over.

Okay, I'll call you tomorrow . . .

She held the sign up to the window. Mick's face beamed, then disappeared.

'After all,' Alex sighed, picking up her juggling balls and tossing them gently into the air, 'I don't want to be like Emma. She never waited to hear why she had been betrayed. Maybe he had a reason. Maybe he was sorry.'

'We'll really have to block up that window,' Jo said. 'Meanwhile, I'm going to let Avalanche out.'

She disappeared up the basement steps. They heard the scurry of Ava's four feet on the floor above, a desperate scramble at the door, then shouting.

'Down girl. Good dog. DOWN!'

'That'll fix *him*.' Jo smiled in a satisfied way. 'But just to make sure, Charlie, put your mirror up in the window. That way if Mick comes back, he'll just see his own ugly face.'

'Now,' said Louise,' tell us the rest.'

One last time, the four friends huddled in the candle's glow to listen to Jo's soft, fascinating voice.

Diana was right. They never returned to the old stone mansion on the river. They moved back to the city so that Daniel could get the treatment he needed. Diana was sick with the same fever for a week, but Rosie, amazingly, escaped.

The estate on the Hudson River was sold to land developers for a pile of money. It turned out that was why Adam's mother was so anxious to get her hands on it.

She didn't want to live there. She wanted to get rich.

Diana's father slowly got well, and he was able to go back to work. After awhile, even thunderstorms didn't bother him.

There was only one sad thing – and Diana never knew what to think about it. Granny Martin had died the night of the storm. They found her the next morning in her cottage by the river, dead of heart failure.

She might have been a ghost after all, Diana always thought, come to help her in her battle with Emma. After all, Emma always listened to Granny, even when she was alive. It was the kind of thing you could never prove, one way or the other.

Seven years later, Diana went to college in a town along the Hudson. When she walked into her first class, she saw a familiar face. A tall, slim young man with a shy smile came over to shake her hand. She knew at once it was Adam.

'He's my Uncle Adam, now. He and Diana got married after they graduated,' Jo added.

'That's great,' Charlie said. 'I guess I'll have to stop suspecting him, seeing as he is your uncle.'

'So Diana's family got rich,' Louise sighed.

'That was wonderful, when they'd been poor for so long.'

'They weren't really *rich*,' Jo said. 'But you're right. They didn't have to worry about money. When Daniel got better they moved to a quiet town and bought a comfortable old house. Diana still visits her brother Daniel, who is grown up, with two kids of his own and a St Bernard puppy . . .'

'Wait a minute!' Louise cried. 'Your dad's first name is Dan. You mean . . . he was . . .' Louise was so excited she could hardly talk.

'That's right,' Jo gave her funny little smile. 'The baby was my dad.'

'Whew!' Charlie threw out her arms. 'Neat! But the whole thing still could have been staged, by Adam's mother, or somebody else. You have to admit it.'

'You go right ahead thinking there was no ghost,' Jo said. 'As for me, I'm convinced. I'm just not sure Emma's ghost was totally evil. In the end, she might have decided to help Diana. After all, they looked so much alike.'

'That reminds me,' Alex said. 'Pull back your hair, Jo.'

'I don't think you want me to do that,' Jo's voice got very deep and scary.

135

She bent her head down, then flipped it back, holding her hair tight.

'Look! It's the *widow's peak*!' shrieked Charlie.

'Oh, Jo, don't!' Louise gasped. 'I'm never going to sleep all night.'

'Who wants to sleep?' Charlie laughed. 'We've got lots of food left. Anybody else got a good story?'

'I think we've had enough stories for one night,' Alex yawned.

'We'll have to have another sleepover. Whose turn next?' Jo asked, shaking her hair loose and returning to her normal voice.

'Well,' said Louise. 'Jo's story reminds me of one I heard.' She shivered. 'It might be even scarier.'

'Let's save it for next time,' Jo said. 'Maybe we should blow out the candles . . .'

'All that storytelling wore you out,' Charlie laughed.

'I don't *want* to go to sleep,' Jo retorted. 'But in case we do, I promised my parents we wouldn't leave the candles burning.'

'All right. One – two – three, blow!' Charlie sang out. There were four puffs and the candle flames flickered out. Only Ajax the cat's eyes glowed in the dark.

'Oooh, it's so dark!' Louise's voice came

through the blackness. It was the first time they'd been in the dungeon with no light.

'Reach out and hold hands,' Jo muttered sleepily from her cosy sleeping bag. 'We can keep talking . . . we don't have to go to sleep . . .'

There were murmurs and sighs in the darkness. 'Do you think Mick really doesn't . . . care about Sonia?' Alex yawned, at last.

There was no answer, but Charlie squeezed one hand, and Jo squeezed the other. In a moment they were all asleep.

THE HAUNTED HOTEL SLEEPOVER

Sharon Siamon

Fading footsteps scare Louise . . .

Cocooned above the city streets, the Sleepover gang pull the curtains tight and settle down with their duvets, ready to listen. Louise has a terrifying tale to tell. Will it spook strong-willed Jo, haunt fun-loving Alex or hold the attention of muddle-headed Charlie? It's time to find out . . .

THE SNOWED-IN SLEEPOVER

Sharon Siamon

A wolf's howl starts Alex's story . . .

Sheltering from the wind in an old log-cabin, the Sleepover gang huddle round a blazing fire, ready to listen. Alex has a mysterious story to tell. Will it capture Jo's imagination, terrify tearful Louise or fascinate her friend Charlie? It's time to find out . . .

ORDER FORM

THE SLEEPOVER SERIES
Sharon Siamon

☐	0 340 67276 5	THE SECRET ROOM SLEEPOVER	£3.50
☐	0 340 67277 3	THE SNOWED-IN SLEEPOVER	£3.50
☐	0 340 67278 1	THE HAUNTED HOTEL SLEEPOVER	£3.50
☐	0 340 67279 1	THE CAMP FIRE SLEEPOVER	£3.50

All Hodder Children's books are available at your local bookshop or newsagent, or can be ordered direct from the publisher. Just tick the titles you want and fill in the form below. Prices and availability subject to change without notice.

Please enclose a cheque or postal order made payable to Bookpoint Ltd to the value of the cover price and allow the following for postage and packing: UK & BFPO: £1.00 for the first book, 50p for the second book, and 30p for each additional book ordered up to a maximum charge of £3.00.
OVERSEAS & EIRE: £2.00 for the first book, £1.00 for the second book, and 50p for each additional book.

Name ....

Address ....

....

....

If you would prefer to pay by credit card, please complete:
Please debit my Visa/Access/Diner's Card/American Express (delete as applicable) card no:

Signature ....

Expiry Date ....

Send to: Hodder Children's Books, Cash Sales Department, Bookpoint, 39 Milton Park, Abingdon, OXON, OX14 4TD, UK. If you have a credit card you may order by telephone. Our direct line is *01235 400414* (lines open 9.00 am – 6.00 pm Monday to Saturday, 24 hour message answering service). Alternatively you can send a fax on *01235 400454*.